Daughters of Destiny

Daughters of Destiny

L. Frank Baum

MINT EDITIONS

Daughters of Destiny was first published in 1906.

This edition published by Mint Editions 2021.

ISBN 9781513211794 | E-ISBN 9781513210599

Published by Mint Editions®

 MINT
EDITIONS

minteditionbooks.com

Publishing Director: Jennifer Newens
Design & Production: Rachel Lopez Metzger
Project Manager: Micaela Clark
Typesetting: Westchester Publishing Services

Contents

BOOK I—THE MAN

    I. PRINCE KASAM OF BALUCHISTAN   9

    II. THE AMERICAN COMMISSION   13

    III. THE PERSIAN PHYSICIAN   22

    IV. THE DAUGHTER OF THE VIZIER   26

    V. THE PERIL OF BURAH KHAN   31

    VI. THE MAN OF DESTINY   36

    VII. DIRRAG   41

    VIII. A WOMAN'S WAY   53

    IX. THE SIXTH DAY   57

    X. AHMED KHAN   62

BOOK II—THE WOMAN

    XI. CAPTURE OF DAVID THE JEW   73

    XII. THE GIRL ON THE DIVAN   82

    XIII. A WILD WOOING   90

    XIV. THE VEILED WOMAN   97

    XV. SALAMAN   101

    XVI. THE ABDUCTION   105

XVII. David Sells an Important Secret   108

XVIII. The Vizier Opens the Gate   115

XIX. In the Garden of Agahr   122

XX. The Girl in the Harem   126

XXI. The Chamber of Death   132

XXII. By the Hand of Allah   134

XXIII. The Vengeance of Maie   139

XXIV. The Spirit of Unrest   141

XXV. Kasam Khan   144

XXVI. Her Serene Highness the Khanum   148

BOOK I
THE MAN

I

Prince Kasam of Baluchistan

"What country did you say, Prince?"

"Baluchistan, my lord."

The great financier lay back in his chair and a slight smile flickered over his stern features. Then he removed his eye-glasses and twirled them thoughtfully around his finger as he addressed the young man opposite.

"I remember," said he, "that when I attended school as a boy one of my chiefest trials in geography was to learn how to bound Baluchistan."

"Ah, do not say that, sir," exclaimed Prince Kasam, eagerly. "It is a customary thing, whenever my country is mentioned, for an Englishman to refer to his geography. I have borne the slight with rare patience, Lord Marvale, since first I came, a boy, to London; but permit me to say that I expected *you* to be better informed."

"But, why?" asked the nobleman, raising his brows at the retort.

"Because Baluchistan is a great country, sir. You might drop all of England upon one of its plains—and have some trouble to find it again."

Lord Marvale's eyes twinkled.

"And how about London?" he asked. "You have many such cities, I suppose?"

"There is but one London, my lord," answered the young man composedly; "and, to be frank with you, there are few clusters of houses in my country that are worthy the name of cities. We Baluchi are a wild race, as yet untamed by the influence of your western civilization, and those who wander in desert and plain far exceed in numbers the dwellers in towns."

"I am not so ignorant as you may suppose," declared Lord Marvale; "for it is a part of my business training to acquire information concerning all countries of the world, however remote and barbaric they may be. For instance, I know that your country is ruled by the Khan of Kelat, and that the English have established a protectorate over it."

"Kelat!" cried the other, a touch of scorn in his tone; "that, sir, is not Baluchistan at all. It is the country of the Brahoes, a weak and cowardly race that is distinct from the Baluchi, my own people. Small wonder they need the English to protect them! But Kelat, although placed in Baluchistan by your map-makers, is another country altogether, and the unconquered Baluchi owe no allegiance to any nation in the world."

For a time the financier sat silently in his chair. Then he asked:

"You have lived here since childhood, Prince?"

"Since eight years of age, my lord."

"Why were you educated in London, if your people dislike Europeans?"

"For political reasons, sir. I am the sole legitimate descendant of seven generations of Khans of Mekran—rulers of all Baluchistan. But in my grandsire's time our throne was usurped by Keedar Khan, a fierce tribesman who carried all before his mighty sword. His son, Burah Khan, now an old man and in bad health, at present rules at Mekran. Therefore I was sent by my kinsmen, who are yet powerful and loyal to our family, to London, that I might escape assassination at the hands of the usurpers."

"I see; you hope to succeed Burah Khan."

"That is my ambition. All that stands in my way is a son of the khan, who, however, has been confined in a Sunnite monastery since youth and is reported to be more fitted to become a priest than a ruler of men."

"Well?"

"My lord, I desire your coöperation and assistance. Twice have I secretly revisited Baluchistan, where my uncle is vizier to the present khan. The adherents to my cause are many. We have no money, but possess vast store of rare jewels, and much gold and silver plate hoarded for centuries—since the day when Alexander's army, marching through our land, was forced to abandon and cast aside much of its burden of plunder. If we can convert this treasure into money it is our intention to hire an army of Afghan mercenaries to assist us and with their aid to rise at the death of Burah Khan, which cannot be long delayed, and again seize the throne that by right belongs to me. You, my lord, are noted for your shrewdness in financing great affairs. Here is one of magnitude in which you may profit largely. Will you aid me?"

The man appealed to was, through long experience, a competent judge of human nature, and while Kasam spoke he studied the young Oriental critically.

The prince was of medium height, full faced and broad shouldered. His beard was clipped in modern fashion, and he wore a conventional frock coat. But his swarthy skin and glittering dark eyes proclaimed his Eastern origin, and for head-dress he wore the turban of his tribe, twisted gracefully but with studied care into that particular fold which to an Oriental declared as plainly as the written page of a book the wearer's nationality and tribe and degree. To the Westerner a turban means nothing more than a head-covering; to the Oriental it is eloquent of detail. In the manner of fold, the size, the color and the material of which it is composed, he reads clearly the wearer's caste and condition in life, and accords him the exact respect that is his due.

Aside from the turban, Kasam wore the tribal sash over his shoulder, thus combining the apparel of the orient with that of the Occident in a picturesque and most effective manner.

The expression of his face was animated and winning; he gesticulated freely, but with grace; the words that flowed from his full red lips were fervent, but well chosen.

Prince Kasam spoke fluent English. His handsome countenance glowed with the eager enthusiasm of youth, with the conscious pride of high station, of powerful friends and of a just cause.

Lord Marvale was impressed.

"Come to me in three days," said the banker. "I will make enquiries and take counsel with my colleagues. Then I shall be able to consider your proposal with more intelligence."

Three days later a long conference was held in Lord Marvale's office, during which Prince Kasam related with clearness yet characteristic Eastern loquaciousness the details of a carefully planned conspiracy to replace him upon the throne of his ancestors. The plot seemed both simple and practical, and Lord Marvale was by no means averse to acquiring the rare treasure of ancient plate and the rich oriental jewels that the adherents of Prince Kasam were anxious to exchange for English money and support.

It was not the only conference before the bargain was finally struck, but Kasam's proposals met with no serious opposition and it was arranged that he should secretly return to Baluchistan, get together the treasure, and bring it with him to London, where Lord Marvale would convert it into money and also negotiate with the Afghans for an army of mercenaries. The countenance and moral support of the English government the banker could safely pledge.

It did not occur to Kasam that time might become a powerful factor in his future plans, and that all this detail would require considerable time to consummate. He had worn out many years of tedious waiting in

London, and really thought events were beginning to move swiftly. But when he received a message stating that Burah Khan was failing fast and urging him to hasten home, he realized that in order to accomplish his purposes he must lose no single moment in delay. Therefore he hurried to Lord Marvale with the information that he would return at once to Baluchistan.

"Good!" exclaimed the banker. "Your decision will relieve me of a slight embarrassment and enable me, through your courtesy, to serve an influential friend."

"That will please me very much," said Kasam.

"There has arrived in London a party of American capitalists representing a great New York syndicate, and our minister in Washington has given their chief a letter to me, asking me to arrange for the safe conduct of the party through Baluchistan."

"Baluchistan! My own country? Why, my lord, few Englishmen have ever approached its borders, and never an American—so far as I know. What can induce them to visit Baluchistan?"

"I understand it is a matter of some railway enterprise or other. These Americans penetrate into the most outlandish and unfrequented places, and no one ever pays much attention to their wanderings. But the minister's letter asks me to supply them with a guide. What do you say, Prince, to undertaking the task yourself? It will enable you to return to Mekran incognito, as the conductor of a party of wealthy and influential Americans; and, as you are not likely to be recognized, you may accomplish your task of collecting the treasure more safely than if you travelled alone."

"That is true," answered the young man, thoughtfully; and after a moment's reflection he added: "Very well; inform your Americans that I will guide them to Baluchistan—even to the walls of Mekran—and no one can do it more safely or swiftly than I."

II

The American Commission

When the American Construction Syndicate, of New York and Chicago, conceived the idea of laying a railway across Baluchistan, through the Alexandrian Pass and so into the Lower Indies—thus connecting Asia and Europe by the shortest possible route—it was regarded as a bold undertaking even for this gigantic corporation. But the Syndicate scorned the imputation that any undertaking might be too hazardous or difficult for it to accomplish; so, when the route was proposed and its advantages understood, the railway was as good as built, in the minds of the directors.

There were preliminaries, of course. A commission must be sent to Baluchistan to secure right of way. And the route must be surveyed. But these were mere matters of detail. Already the Syndicate had built a road across the Balkans; even now it was laying rails in Turkestan. And this Baluchistan route was but a part of a great system wisely and cleverly projected.

The Alexandrian Pass was the same that nearly proved fatal to Alexander the Great on the occasion of his invasion of India. Since then little had been heard of it. But doubtless the Pass was still there, and had been waiting all these years for someone to utilize it. It was part of the domain of the Khan of Mekran, who also ruled the greater part of Baluchistan.

The directors had the histories consulted. Baluchistan seemed practically unknown to history. There were no books of travel in Baluchistan. Strange! The country was there—very big on the maps—and someone ought to know something about it. But no one apparently did.

Well, the Commission would discover all there was to know, and a semi-barbarous country would be easy to deal with.

Next the Commission itself was considered, and Colonel Piedmont Moore was selected as its chief. Colonel Moore was one of the Syndicate's largest stockholders and most respected officers, and the gentleman himself directed the selection of the chief, because he had decided to get away from the office for a time and travel, his health having become undermined by too close attention to business.

Dr. Warner, his intimate friend, had repeatedly counselled him to break away from work and take better care of himself. Travel was what he needed—travel in such remote lands that no temptation would exist to return to New York to "see how the Syndicate was getting on."

When the Baluchistan Commission was first spoken of the Colonel mentioned it to his old friend, who was also a stockholder in the concern, the doctor having grown wealthy and retired from active practice several years before.

"Just the thing!" declared the old gentleman. "A trip to Baluchistan would probably set you on your feet again. Let me see—where is it? Somewhere in South America, isn't it?"

"No; I believe it's in Asia," returned the Colonel, gravely. "And that is a long distance to journey alone."

"Why, bless your soul! I'll go with you," declared Dr. Warner, cheerfully. "I've intended to do a bit of travelling myself, as soon as I got around to it; and Baluchistan has a fine climate, I'm sure."

"No one seems to know much about it," answered the Colonel.

"All the better! Why, we'll be explorers. We'll find out all about Darkest Baluchistan, and perhaps write a book on our discoveries. We'll combine business and pleasure. I'm in the Syndicate. Have me appointed as your second on the Commission, and the Syndicate shall pay our expenses."

So the plans were made, and afterward amplified to include the Colonel's son, Mr. Allison Moore, as official surveyor. Not that Allison Moore was an especially practical or proficient man in his profession—indeed, the directors feared just the contrary was true—but this was going to be a sort of family party, and the Colonel was a person absolutely to be depended upon. He was willing to vouch for his son, and that settled the matter.

In fact, the Colonel was glad to have Allison with him on this trip. Glad to have the young man under his eye, for one thing, and glad of an opportunity to advance his son professionally. For Allison seemed to have some difficulty in getting the right sort of a start, even though he had spent years in making the attempt.

At first the young man declined to go to Baluchistan, and there were angry words between father and son. But Dr. Warner acted as peacemaker and Allison finally consented to go provided his father would pay certain debts he had accumulated and make him an allowance in addition to his salary from the syndicate. It was the first salary he had ever received, and although the syndicate thought it liberal enough, it seemed absurdly small to a gentleman of Allison's requirements.

All this having been pleasantly settled, the doctor proposed taking along his daughter Bessie, who had been pleading to go ever since the trip was suggested.

At first the Colonel demurred.

"It's a business expedition," said he.

"Business and pleasure," amended the doctor, promptly.

"And I don't know what sort of country we're going to. It may not be pleasant for ladies."

"We'll make it pleasant for them. Better take Janet with you, Colonel, and we'll induce Aunt Lucy to go along as chaperon."

"She wouldn't consider such a trip an instant."

"Who wouldn't?"

"Janet."

"Ask her about it."

So the Colonel mentioned it at dinner, in a casual way, and Miss Janet Moore at first opened her beautiful dark eyes in surprise, then considered the matter silently for a half hour, and at dessert decided she would go.

The Colonel was pleased. It was difficult to interest Janet in anything, and if the Baluchistan trip would draw her out of her dreamy lassitude and awaken in her something of her old bright self, why, the syndicate be thanked for conceiving the idea of a Commission!

The old gentleman tolerated his son as a cross to be borne with Christian resignation: he was devoted to his beautiful daughter.

Janet Moore in face and form represented that type of American girl which has come to be acknowledged in all countries the ideal of womanly grace and loveliness. The delicate contour of her features did not destroy nor even abate their unmistakable strength and dignity. The well-opened eyes were clear as a mountain pool, yet penetrating and often discomfiting in their steadiness; the mouth was wide, yet sweet and essentially feminine; the chin, held high and firm, was alluringly curved and dimpled, displaying beneath it a throat so rarely perfect that only in the Sicilian Aphrodite has sculptor ever equalled it. Her head was poised in queenly fashion upon a form so lithe and rounded that Diana might well have envied it, and while Janet's expression at all times bore a trace of sadness, a half smile always lingered upon her lips—a smile so pathetic in its appeal that one who loved her would be far less sympathetically affected by a flood of tears. The girl had suffered a terrible disappointment seven years before. The man she loved had been proven an arrant scoundrel. He had forged her father's name; been guilty of crime and ingratitude; worse than all else, he had run away to escape punishment. It had been clearly proven against Herbert Osborne, yet Janet, by a strange caprice, would never accept the proof. She had a distinctly feminine idea that in spite of everything Herbert was incapable of crime or any sort of dishonesty. And, knowing full well that she stood alone in her belief, the girl proudly suffered in silence.

There was more to Janet's old romance than anyone ever dreamed; but whatever the girl's secret might be, she kept all details safely locked within her own bosom.

The Colonel was surprised that his daughter should so readily agree to undertake a tedious and perhaps uninteresting journey to a far-away country; but he was nevertheless delighted. The change would assuredly do her good, and Bessie Warner was just the jolly companion she needed to waken her into new life.

So the doctor was informed that the two girls would accompany the Commission, and Bessie at once set out to interview her Aunt Lucy and persuade that very accommodating lady to go with them as chaperon. Aunt Lucy was without a single tie to keep her in New York, and she was so accustomed to being dragged here and there by her energetic niece that she never stopped to enquire where Baluchistan was or how they were expected to get there. In her mild and pleasant little voice she remarked:

"Very well, dear. When do we start?"

"Oh, I'll send you word, auntie. And thank you very much for being so nice."

"We'll be back by Thanksgiving, I suppose?"

"I hardly know, dear. It's a business trip of papa's, and of course the length of our stay depends entirely upon him and the Colonel, who is some way interested in the matter. By the way, it's called a Commission, and we'll be very important travellers, I assure you! Goodbye, auntie, dear!"

Then she hurried away; for that suggestion of returning by Thanksgiving day, scarcely a month distant, showed her how little Aunt Lucy really knew of the far journey she had so recklessly undertaken.

So this was the personnel of the famous Commission that was to invade Baluchistan and secure from the Khan of Mekran a right of way for a railroad through the Alexandrian Pass: Col. Piedmont Moore, Chief; Dr. Luther Warner, Assistant; Allison Moore, Civil Engineer; Janet Moore and Bessie Warner, chaperoned by Mrs. Lucy Higgins, Accessories and Appendages.

The Commission crossed the ocean in safety; it reached London without incident worthy of record, and there the Chief endeavored to secure some definite knowledge of Baluchistan.

Not until he had presented the British minister's letter to Lord Marvale did the Colonel meet with any good fortune in his quest. Then the atmosphere of doubt and uncertainty suddenly cleared, for a real Baluch of Baluchistan was then in London and could be secured to pilot the Americans to their destination.

To be sure this native—Kasam Ullah Raab by name—was uncommunicative at first regarding the character of the Khan of Mekran or the probability of the Syndicate's being able to negotiate for a right of way through his country; and, indeed, the Baluch could be induced to commit himself neither to criticism nor encouragement of the plan. But, after all, it was not to be supposed that much information of value could be secured from a mere guide. The main point to be considered just then was how to journey to Mekran with comfort and despatch, and incidentally the accomplishments and attainments of the guide himself.

Kasam's charming manners and frank, handsome countenance soon won the confidence of the entire party. Even Allison Moore did not withhold his admiration for the "gentlemanly barbarian," as Aunt Lucy called him, and the young ladies felt entirely at ease in his company.

"Really," said Bessie, "our Kasam is quite a superior personage, for a guide."

And the prince overheard the remark and smiled.

During the journey the guide proved very thoughtful and gallant toward the young ladies, and with the friendly familiarity common to Americans they made Kasam one of themselves and treated him with frank consideration. It was perhaps natural that the prince should respond by openly confiding to them his rank and ambition, thus explaining his reason for journeying with them in the humble capacity of guide. Before they had reached Quettah the entire party knew every detail of Kasam's history, and canvassed his prospect of becoming khan as eagerly as they did the details of their own vast enterprise. Indeed, the Colonel was quick to recognize the advantage the Commission would acquire by being on friendly terms with the future Khan of Mekran, and since Burah Khan was old and suffered from many wounds received in many battles, the chances were strongly in favor of the young prince being soon called to the throne.

"My uncle is vizier to the usurper," said Kasam, "and I will secure, through him, an interview for you with Burah Khan. Also my uncle shall extend to your party his good offices. He is the leader of the party which is plotting to restore to me the throne of my ancestors, and is therefore entirely devoted to my interests. Of course you will understand that I dare not publicly announce my presence in Mekran; therefore I will guide you as a hired servant, and so escape notice. Only my uncle Agahr and two of the sirdars—or leaders of the tribes—are acquainted with my person or know who I really am. But the spies of the Khan are everywhere, as I have discovered during my former secret visits to Mekran, and it is best for me to avoid them at this juncture."

All this was intensely interesting to every member of the Commission, and it is no wonder Bessie smiled upon the handsome guide who possessed so romantic a story. But Bessie's brightest smiles seemed less desirable to Kasam than one sympathetic look from Janet's Moore's serious dark eyes.

The evident adoration with which the "foreign prince," as she called him, came to regard Miss Moore was a source of much uneasiness to Aunt Lucy; but Janet did not seem to notice it, and the young man was ever most humble and discreet while in her presence. In fact, there was nothing in the prince's behavior that the gentle old lady might complain of openly. Yet she had her own suspicions, clinched by experienced observation, of the foreigner's intentions, and determined to keep a sharp lookout in the interests of her charge. Soon they would enter a barbarous country where this handsome prince would be more powerful than the great Commission itself. And then?

At Quettah they secured camels and formed a caravan to cross the corner of the Gedrasian Desert and so journey on to Mekran; but there was more or less grumbling when this necessity was disclosed. Allison Moore, who had behaved fairly well so far, flatly declined to go further toward the wild and unknown country they had come so far to visit. The inn at Quettah was fairly good. He would stay there. Vainly his father stormed and argued, alternately; he even threatened to cut his son off with a dime—the nearest approach to the legendary shilling he could think of; but Allison proved stubborn. Having once declared his intention, he answered nothing to the demands of his father or the pleadings of Dr. Warner. He smoked his pipe, stared straight ahead and would not budge an inch from Quettah.

"I'll wait here till you come back," he said, sullenly. "If you ever do."

This was the first disagreeable incident of the journey. Even Bessie was depressed by Allison's inference that they were involved in a dangerous enterprise. As for Aunt Lucy, she suddenly conceived an idea that the band of Afghans Kasam had employed to accompany the caravan were nothing more than desperate bandits, who would carry the Commission into the mountains and either murder every individual outright or hold them for an impossible ransom.

Kasam's earnest protestations finally disabused the minds of the ladies of all impressions of danger. It was true that in Baluchistan they might meet with lawless bands of Baluchi; but their caravan was too well guarded to be interfered with. They were supplied with fleet saddle horses and fleeter dromedaries; the twenty Afghans were bold and fearless and would fight for them unto death. Really, they had nothing at all to fear.

So at last they started, an imposing cavalcade, for the Khan's dominions, leaving Allison in the doorway of the inn smoking his everlasting pipe and staring sullenly after them. The ladies rode dromedaries, and found them less uncomfortable than they had at first feared they would be. The Colonel did not seem to mind his son's desertion, for Kasam had whispered in his ear an amusing plan to conquer the young surveyor's obstinacy.

An hour later one of the prince's Afghans, selected because he spoke the English language, returned from the caravan to warn Allison that he was in grave danger. The night before a plot had been overheard to murder and rob the young man as soon as his friends had departed.

"If you shoot well and are quick with the knife," added the Afghan, coolly, "you may succeed in preserving your life till our return. His Highness the Prince sent me to advise you to fight to the last, for these scoundrels of Quettah have no mercy on foreigners."

Then Allison stared again, rather blankly this time, and the next moment requested the Afghan to secure him a horse.

Kasam was assuring the Colonel for the twentieth time that his son would soon rejoin them when Allison and the Afghan rode up at a gallop and attached themselves without a word to the cavalcade.

And the Colonel was undecided whether most to commend the guide's cunning or his son's cautiousness.

This portion of their journey was greatly enjoyed by all members of the party. The doctor declared he felt more than ever like an explorer, and the Colonel silently speculated on all that might be gained by opening this unknown territory to the world by means of the railway. The distinct novelty of their present mode of progression was delightful to the ladies, and Aunt Lucy decided she much preferred a camel to an automobile. Even Janet's pale cheeks gathered a tint from the desert air, and despite the uncertainties of their pilgrimage the entire party retained to a wonderful degree their cheerfulness and good nature.

At the end of four days they halted in a small village where Kasam intended them to rest while he alone went forward to Mekran to obtain their passports. For they were now upon the edge of the Khan's dominions, and without Burah's protection the party was liable to interference by some wandering tribe of Baluchi.

The accommodations they were able to secure in this unfrequented village were none of the best, and Allison began to grumble anew, thereby bringing upon himself a stern rebuke from the guide, who frankly informed the young man that he was making his friends uncomfortable when nothing could be gained by protesting.

"You cannot go back, and you dare not go forward without passports," said Kasam. "Therefore, if you possess any gentlemanly instincts at all, you will endeavor to encourage the ladies and your father, instead of adding to their annoyance. When one travels, one must be a philosopher."

"You are impertinent," returned Allison, scowling.

"If I yielded to my earnest desire," said the prince, "I would ask my men to flog you into a decent frame of mind. If I find, when I return, that you have been disagreeable, perhaps I shall punish you in that way. It may be well for you to remember that we are no longer in Europe."

The young man made no reply, but Kasam remembered the vengeful look that flashed from his eyes.

Heretofore the prince had worn the European frock coat; now he assumed the white burnous of his countrymen. When he came to bid adieu to his employers before starting for Mekran, Bessie declared that their guide looked more handsome and distinguished than ever—"just like that famous picture of the Son of the Desert, you know."

Kasam was about to mount his horse—a splendid Arabian he had purchased in the village—when a tall Baluch who was riding by cast a shrewd glance into the young man's face, sharply reined in his stallion, and placed a thumb against his forehead, bowing low.

Kasam's brown face went ashen grey. He gazed steadily into the stranger's eyes.

"You are bound for Mekran, my prince?" asked the tall Baluch, in the native tongue.

"I ride at once."

"Make all haste possible. Burah Khan is dying."

"Dying? Blessed Allah!" cried Kasam, striking his forehead in despair. "Burah Khan dying, and our plans still incomplete! I have waited too long."

"Perhaps not," retorted the other, significantly. "It is a lingering disease, and you may yet get to Mekran in time."

"In time? In time for what?" asked Kasam.

"To strike!"

Kasam stared at him. The tall Baluch smiled and shook the rein over his horse's ears.

"I am of the tribe of Raab, my prince. May Allah guide you to success."

Kasam did not reply. His head rested against the arched neck of his horse, and his form shook with a slight nervous tremor. But next moment he stood erect. The dazed look inspired by the bitter news he had heard was giving way to his old eager, cheery expression.

"All is not lost!" he said, speaking aloud. "Fate knocks, and I will throw open the door. Allah grant that Burah Khan lives until I reach Mekran!"

He sprang to the saddle, put spurs to his steed and dashed away at full speed into the desert.

"I hope," said the Colonel, looking after him anxiously, "that nothing has gone wrong."

III

The Persian Physician

Burah Khan, known as the Lion of Mekran, Headsman of the Nine Tribes of Baluchi and Defender of the Faith, was, without doubt, a very sick man.

He lay upon a divan in the courtyard of his palace, propped with silken cushions redolent of the odors of musk. The waters of the fountain that splashed at his side were also scented with musk, and the heavy and stifling perfume permeated the entire atmosphere of the court. At the head of the divan sat a girl, indolently waving a fan above the head of the Khan. Not far from his feet a white-bearded man squatted upon a rug and eyed the sick one with curious intentness. This was Agahr, the vizier. Behind him sat a group of officers and sirdars, silently watching the scene.

Burah Khan, despite his sad condition, was fully clothed in his customary regalia. He wore a waistcoat of dingy white plush upon which were sewn enough rubies to have ransomed a kingdom. His yellow satin trousers were soiled and crumpled. The long outer robe was of faded rose-color and had nine stars, formed of clustered diamonds, down the front. The deep collar was stiff with masses of the same precious gems. The entire dress seemed as tawdry as a circus costume at the end of the season; but it was of enormous value, and the Khan, with oriental love of magnificence, clung to it even as he lay upon his death-bed.

He was a notable character, this Burah Khan, son of the terrible Keedar Khan who had conquered all of Baluchistan and ruled it with a rod of iron. Burah had inherited with the throne the fierce hatred with which his father was ever regarded; yet he had not only held every province secure, but had won the respect and fear of all his people. The thirty years of his rule had not been void of wars and bloodshed, yet at the head of his nine Baluch tribes the Khan had swept aside all opposition and won for himself the title of "The Lion of Mekran," Mekran being his dwelling-place when not in the saddle.

Today, gaunt and haggard, he lay gasping upon his divan. His fingers opened and closed convulsively in the meshes of his iron-gray beard; his drooping eyelids were sunk in deep sockets. The pallor of death showed through his swarthy skin. To Agahr and the silent group behind him it seemed that the Khan was conquered at last.

The sick one moved restlessly and raised his hand.

"Has—has—he come?" he asked, speaking the words with much difficulty.

Agahr leaned forward, without rising, and answered his master with composure:

"Not yet, lord."

It was a question often repeated and as often answered with the same words.

A moan came from the Khan. The vizier noted the patient's restlessness and made a sign with his hand. At once the curtains of the rear entrance were swept aside and a troop of girls entered. They were robed in white; vines of the mountain iral were twined in their hair; in their hands were bellalas. The girls danced. A tall Arab with immense hoops of gold in his ears beat a tambo to mark the time, and the bellalas chimed a tinkling chorus.

The eyes of the Khan never opened, but he made an impatient gesture and moaned again. The intent Agahr noted this and at his command the noise of the tambo ceased and the girls withdrew. Evidently the Khan could no longer be amused in this fashion.

For a brief space of time the courtyard again became silent. Then, so suddenly that a thrill crept over the watchers, a tall imposing figure glided to the side of the divan and cast a shadow over the face of the sick man.

Burah Khan moved, opened his eyes and fixed his gaze eagerly upon the new arrival. The vizier arose quickly and approached the couch, bowing low and looking into the calm countenance of the stranger with undisguised anxiety. The group of minor officials also looked their interest, and the girl forgot to wave her fan while she examined the person of the man so long awaited.

"The great physician is here, my master," whispered the vizier. But Burah Khan did not heed him. An expression of relief had come to his pinched features, and his eyes were fixed earnestly upon the face bent above him, as if he would read his fate in the countenance of the famous Persian who had been brought all the way from Kelat to minister to his imperative needs.

The physician raised the sick man's eyelids and glanced beneath them. He placed his right hand under the Khan's head and at the same time pressed an ear to his chest. It seemed enough. He stood erect, with folded arms, bending a searching yet kindly gaze upon the face upturned to his.

"Tell me!" pleaded the Khan, feebly.

The Persian gave a quick glance around. Then he answered:

"They listen."

"Let them hear," said the Khan, raising himself with an effort upon his elbow. "They—are all—friends."

A queer look came over the stranger's face. But he said, in a calm voice:

"The sickness is fatal. You will die."

For a moment the Lion of Mekran returned the other's gaze steadily. Then he lay back upon his pillows and sighed.

Agahr, who eyed his master as if fascinated, heaved an echoing sigh, and the group of officials exchanged looks of consternation.

"When?" asked the Khan, his voice now strong and clear, his eyes on the impassive face before him.

"A day—an hour," replied the Persian, slowly. "It is Death's secret."

For a few moments the silence was unbroken save for the splash of the fountain as its perfumed spray fell into the marble basin. Then the Khan again aroused himself.

"Can you hold Death at bay—for a time?" he asked.

"How long?"

"Speak, Agahr!" turning to his vizier. "How long to get my son here—to assemble the Sirdars of the Nine Tribes?"

Agahr was trembling visibly. He clasped and unclasped his thin hands nervously and glanced first at his master and then at the physician.

"Speak!" said the latter, sternly.

"To the monastery of Takkatu is three days' journey—three days, at least," he said, hesitatingly. "And for Prince Ahmed to return will require three more. Seven days—a week—with fast riding."

"Then," said the Khan, calmly, "they must ride fast." He turned to the Persian. "Can you fight Death so long?"

The Persian nodded. The pluck of Burah Khan aroused his admiration.

"I will fight Death so long," said he, gravely.

"And the sirdars?" asked the sick man, once more turning to his vizier.

"They can be assembled in five days," answered Agahr, after a moment's reflection. "Three are already here."

"Good!" declared the Khan. "Let Dirrag ride within the hour."

"For the sirdars?"

"For Ahmed."

He fell back again, and a man rose from the group behind Agahr and with an obeisance toward the divan glided swiftly from the courtyard.

The physician, noting the action, turned to the vizier.

"Dirrag?" he enquired.

"Dirrag," responded the other, mechanically.

The Persian gave his patient a sharp scrutiny, and drawing a phial from his bosom placed it to the now colorless lips of the Khan.

"Clear the place," he commanded Agahr, and without awaiting a response himself stepped quickly through the outer arch.

Outside Dirrag was mounting a strong Arabian mare. The Persian arrested him with a gesture.

"The Prince must be here in six days," he said, in a low but commanding voice. "Six days, or—"

"I understand," said Dirrag, and put spurs to the mare.

IV

The Daughter of the Vizier

Upon a stone gallery overlooking the courtyard of a handsome dwelling not far from the palace of the khan reclined a girl, beautiful with that mysterious Eastern beauty that has been for ages the despair of poets and artists and which attains its full charm only in the Orient. She was scarcely seventeen years of age, yet her rounded outlines, her graceful poise, her sedate demeanor, all proclaimed her a maiden on the verge of womanhood. Her eyes, round and soft as those of a fawn, were absolutely inscrutable; her features in repose held the immutable expression of the Sphynx. When she smiled sunbeams danced in her eyes and a girlish dimple showed in her chin. But she rarely smiled. The composed, serious, languorous expression dominated her exquisite face.

The girl was richly dressed. Her silken gown was of finest texture; pearls of rare size were twined in her dark hair; a golden serpent whose every scale was a lustrous diamond spanned her waist; upon her breast glittered a solitary blood-red ruby of historic fame, known in song and story for generations.

For this maiden was Maie, only daughter of Agahr, Grand Vizier to the Lion of Mekran and to his father before him—the terrible Keedar Khan.

Next to Burah himself in rank, virtually directing all the civic affairs of the nation, responsible to none save his stern master, Agahr was indeed a personage of vast importance in the realm. The sirdars of the nine fighting tribes of Baluchi, the main support of the Khan, might look upon the vizier scornfully; but they obeyed his laws and avoided any interference with his civic functions.

Maie was the daughter of Agahr's old age, his only companion and his constant delight. To her he confided many of the problems that from time to time confronted him, and often a quiet word from the girl's lips showed him the matter in a new light and guided him in his actions. The old man had discovered a store of common sense in the dainty head of his daughter; the inscrutable velvet eyes were wells of wisdom from which he drew solace and counsel in all difficulties.

On the evening of this eventful day came Agahr to the gallery where his daughter reclined. And as he sat beside her she turned her eyes upon his face and seemed to read it clearly.

"The Khan is worse," said she, quietly.

"He is dying," answered the vizier. "The Persian physician has come from Kelat, and he says there is no hope."

"We shall be making history soon," remarked the girl, in soft tones. "The Khan will pass away, and Kasam is here."

The vizier moved uneasily on his seat.

"Kasam is here; yes," said he. "But no one knows the secret save us. No one knows who our Kasam is."

"They will know soon," returned the girl in a calm, expressionless voice. "Our cousin Kasam is rightful heir to the throne—when the Lion's eyes are closed in death."

"You forget that Burah Khan has also a son," said the old man, harshly. "Even now Dirrag is riding full speed to the Sunnite monastery at Takkatu to bring hither the Prince Ahmed."

"That he may be acknowledged successor to the throne by the assembled sirdars of the Nine Tribes?"

"Yes."

"But the Khan is dying. The Prince cannot arrive in time."

"Perhaps not. Yet that accursed Persian has promised to prolong the Khan's life for seven days. If he succeeds—"

The girl bent forward suddenly.

"He must not succeed!" she exclaimed, in a clear voice.

Agahr shrank from the intentness of her gaze.

"Hear me!" she continued. "Kasam is our kinsman; the throne is his by right. Most of our citizens and many of the members of the Nine Tribes secretly favor his claim. A crisis approaches, and we must take advantage of it. The Lion of Mekran must not live seven days. If his son Ahmed, who has been secluded for twenty years in a monastery, and is said to be devoted to Allah, is not here to be recognized as the successor to the throne, the people will acclaim Kasam their khan. It is all very simple, my father. The Lion of Mekran must not live seven days!"

"What, plotting again, cousin?" cried a cheery voice behind them. Agahr gave a sudden start and wheeled around with a frown, meeting the smiling face of Prince Kasam, but the girl moved not even an eyelid.

"Pardon me, uncle, for startling you," said the young man, coming forward and taking a seat beside the vizier. "I arrived in time to hear cousin Maie doom Burah Kahn to an early death, as if the dark angel fought on our side. What a wonderful little conspirator you are, my Maie!"

She looked into his face thoughtfully not caring to acknowledge the compliment of his words or the ardor of his gaze. But Agahr said, gruffly:

"The conspiracies of women cost many men their heads."

"Very true, uncle," replied Kasam, becoming grave. "But we are in sore straights, and a little plotting may not come amiss. If the son of the old Lion—who, by the way, is also my cousin—is acknowledged by the sirdars, he is liable to make a change in his officers. We may lose our vizier, and with the office more than half our power with the people. In that event I can never become kahn."

"The son of Burah must be a weakling and a dreamer," said the girl, thoughtfully. "What can be expected of one who for twenty years has associated with monks and priests?"

"Twenty years?" exclaimed Kasam; "then my cousin Ahmed must be nearly thirty years of age."

"And a recluse," added Maie, quietly. "You, Prince, are not yet twenty-five, and you have lived in the world. We need not, I am sure, fear the gentle son of Burah—even though he be acknowledged by his father and the sirdars of the tribes."

"Which will surely happen if the Khan lives seven days. Is it not so? But if Allah calls him sooner, and my friends are loyal—why, then, I may become khan myself, and much trouble spared. The English have an injunction to 'strike while the iron is hot.' We may safely apply it to ourselves."

Maie glanced at her father, and there was a glint of triumph in the dark eyes.

"It is what I have said," she murmured. "The Lion of Mekran must not live seven days."

"Do you know, fair one," remarked Kasam, lightly, "that only yesterday I bewailed the approaching fate of the usurper, and longed to have him live until we could secure England's support?"

"England!" she cried, scornfully. "What is that far-away nation to our Baluchistan? It is *here* that history will be made."

Kasam laughed merrily.

"What a logical little head you have, cousin!" he answered, laying his hand upon her own, caressingly. "To us, indeed, Baluchistan is the world. And England's help is far away from us in this crisis. Tell me, Maie, what is your counsel?"

"It is your duty, Prince, to prevent Burah Khan from living until his son arrives to be acknowledged his successor."

Kasam's face became suddenly grave.

"*My* duty, cousin?" he replied. "It is no man's duty to murder, even to become khan. But perhaps I misunderstood your words. I am practically a stranger in my own land, and can do little to further my own interests, which naturally include the interests of my friends. If Burah Khan fails to live until his son's arrival it will be through the will of Allah, and by no act of mine."

"You are a coward," said the girl, scornfully.

"Yes," he answered, coldly; "I am afraid to become a murderer."

"Peace, both of you!" commanded the vizier, angrily. "You are like a pair of children. Do you think that I, who have been Burah's faithful officer for thirty years, would countenance treachery or foul play while he lies upon his death-bed? I long to see Prince Kasam seated upon the throne, but it must be through honest diplomacy, and by no assassin's stroke."

"Right, my uncle!" cried Kasam, seizing the vizier's hand in a hearty clasp. "Otherwise, were I khan, you should be no officer of mine."

Agahr and his daughter exchanged a quick glance, and the girl said, languidly:

"I was doubtless wrong, urged on by the intensity of my feeling and my loyalty to the Tribe of Raab. But a woman's way is, I think, more direct and effective than a man's."

"Even if less honest, cousin?" retorted the young man, playfully pinching her cheek. "Let us bide our time and trust to the will of Allah. This evening I must set out on my return to Quanam. What answer shall I take to my foreign friends who await me?"

"Tell me, Kasam; why do they wish to cross our territory—to visit our villages and spy upon our people?" asked Agahr suspiciously.

"It is as I told you, my uncle. They are people of great wealth, from the far western country of America, and it is their custom to penetrate to every part of the world and lay rails of iron over which chariots may swiftly speed. We have no such rails in Baluchistan."

"Nor do we desire them," returned the vizier, brusquely.

"But they would bring to us all the merchandise of that wonderful western world. They would bring us wealth in exchange for our own products," said Kasam, eagerly.

"And they would bring hundreds of infidels to trick and rob us. I know of these railways," declared the vizier.

"I also," answered Kasam, lightly. "I have been educated in Europe, and know well the benefits of western civilization."

"But the Baluchi do not. Our own high and advanced civilization is enough for us."

The young man smiled.

"It is not worth an argument now," he remarked. "The present mission of this party of infidels is to examine our country and consider whether a railway across it would be profitable. All that I now require is a passport and safe conduct for them. It will benefit our cause, as well, for only as the guide to these foreigners dared I return to my native land. If I am permitted to depart tonight with the passport I can easily return in time for the crisis that approaches. Then perhaps our American friends will be of service to us, for no one will suspect their guide of being the exiled heir to the throne."

The vizier hesitated.

"But the railway—"

"Bother the railway!" interrupted Kasam, impatiently. "That is a matter of the future, a matter for the new khan and his vizier to decide upon, whoever they may chance to be."

"Here is the passport," said Agahr, reluctantly drawing a parchment from his breast. "Burah Khan was too sick to be bothered with the request of the infidels, so I made out the paper and signed it by virtue of my office."

"Ah, and affixed the great seal, I perceive," added Kasam, taking the document. "I thank you, uncle Agahr. We shall get along famously together—when I am khan."

He bade them adieu the next moment, embracing the vizier and kissing his cousin's hand with a gallantry that brought a slight flush to the girl's cheeks. And soon they heard the quick beat of his horse's hoofs as he rode away.

Maie and her father looked into each other's eyes. Presently the old man spoke, slowly and thoughtfully.

"You will share his throne, my child."

The girl nodded and fanned herself.

"The life in Europe has made Kasam foolish," said she. Then, leaning forward and regarding the vizier earnestly, she added in a whisper:

"Nevertheless, Burah Khan must not live seven days!"

V

The Peril of Burah Khan

Three days had passed. The khan remained sunk in a stupor caused by the medicines administered by the Persian physician, who hovered constantly around the bedside of his patient. Burah now lay in a well aired, high vaulted chamber. The musk-scented cushions had been ostracised, the dancing girls dismissed. Quiet reigned throughout the vast palace.

Occasionally Agahr would thrust his head through the curtains draping the entrance, as if seeking to know that all was well; but the Persian merely gave him a reassuring nod and motioned him away.

This summary banishment did not please the vizier. His daughter had assisted him in forming several plans of great political import, and the conduct of the foreign physician prevented their being carried to a successful issue.

Thus Agahr, appearing again at the entrance, beckoned with imperative gesture the Persian to join him; and, after a careful inspection of his patient, lying peaceful and unconscious, the physician obeyed.

Together they paced up and down the deserted marble passage, the Persian's quick eye never leaving the entrance to the khan's chamber, while Agahr plied him with eager questions concerning his master's condition.

"He will live until his son, the Prince Ahmed, arrives," said the other, calmly. "He will remain unconscious, but he will live."

"And then?" asked the vizier, anxiously.

"Then I will awaken him. He will have full command of all his faculties for a brief period—and then he will pass away quickly."

Agahr sighed.

"Is it not possible for him to pass away during this stupor?" he enquired.

"Yes, it is possible," answered the Persian. "But I believe I can prevent that. My task requires constant vigilance: that is why I dare not leave the Khan's chamber."

"I will send a man to relieve you," said the vizier. "You can instruct him in his duties and he will be faithful."

"No," returned the Persian.

An awkward silence followed. Then Agahr stopped suddenly and said:

"I will be frank with you. The son of Burah Khan is not the rightful heir to the throne of Mekran. It is the exiled Prince Kasam, from whose grandsire Keedar Khan by right of sword wrested all Baluchistan. Therefore it is best for the country that Burah does not live until his son arrives."

He paused, wiping the perspiration from his brow and glancing half fearfully into the grave face of the physician. The latter nodded.

"I understand," said he.

Agahr became reassured.

"The ancestors of Prince Kasam," he continued, earnestly, "ruled the land for nine generations. Then the Baluchi rebelled and put their Headsman, the fierce Keedar Khan, upon the throne his own brother was forced to vacate. I being at the time vizier, remained Keedar's vizier, as I have remained vizier to his son. By means of wars and bloodshed these terrible men have for forty-six years dominated all Baluchistan. It is now time, in the interest of justice and humanity, that the rightful heir should recover the throne."

"Did not Prince Kasam's ancestors conquer this country with the aid of the Afghans, and put to death every member of the then reigning family?" asked the Persian.

"It is a matter of history," said Agahr, proudly. "They were my ancestors, these bold conquerors, as well as the ancestors of Prince Kasam."

"Yet Keedar Khan made you his vizier, and his son retained you?"

"Yes; and I have been faithful."

"But now, it seems to me, you are speaking treason," said the physician.

"Not so," declared the vizier, indignantly. "Burah Khan, by your own showing, is virtually dead at this moment. I owe no allegiance to his son, whom I have never seen."

"How is that?" asked the physician, in surprise.

"When Ahmed was a child his father, fearing a revolt and that his boy might fall by an assassin's knife, placed him in the Sunnite monastery at Takkatu for safe keeping. There he has remained ever since. It will be necessary for Burah Khan to officially acknowledge him before the chiefs of the Nine Tribes and to appoint him his own successor, before Ahmed can legally occupy the throne. If this is not done the people, who are weary of the rule of these tyrants, will acclaim Kasam as khan."

"But Prince Ahmed will arrive, and be acknowledged. Burah Khan has so willed it, and he is still the master."

Agahr faced the Persian with an angry frown.

"Do you refuse to assist us?" he asked, sharply.

"I refuse to betray the man whose life I have promised to preserve until his son arrives," declared the physician.

"But you are a stranger—a Persian."

"Even so."

"And you expect a reward, or you would not have hastened to Mekran when summoned by the Khan. Name your price. I will double it, and you shall depart this very night."

The Persian smiled.

"Here, and throughout the world," said he, "the strongest argument is the clink of gold. Listen well, your Excellency. I have promised Burah Khan life for seven days. I shall keep my promise. Then, if the Prince does not come, I can do no more."

The vizier started.

"If the Prince does not come?" he repeated, thoughtfully.

"To be sure."

"Ah! I had not thought of that!" exclaimed the old man.

"It is the only thing I fear," said the other, with exasperating coolness; "but I rely upon Dirrag. If you are able to delay him you will doubtless win the throne for Prince Kasam."

Before the mocking tones had died away the physician disappeared behind the draperies of the khan's chamber, and the vizier, controlling his anger and chagrin as best he might, walked away to concoct further plans.

The woman who brought the Persian his evening meal became confused under his sharp scrutiny and started to retire hurriedly. He arrested her with a stern command, saying:

"Sit here and taste of the dish you have brought."

Then she began to tremble.

"Master, I dare not!" she wailed.

"Very well. Take away this food and bring me eggs boiled in the shell."

The physician was bending over the couch of the khan when one of the under cooks entered silently with the eggs. The man was of the Brahoe caste, small and wiry. He placed the eggs upon the table and eyed for a time the back of the tall Persian, who seemed intent upon his patient. But a moment later he suddenly straightened, threw back his hand and caught the wrist of the Brahoe in a firm grasp.

A dagger fell upon the rug, and the man shrank back shuddering before the gleaming eyes of the physician.

An instant they remained motionless. Then, releasing his prisoner, the physician picked up the dagger, placed it within his own bosom and seated himself quietly at the table. One of the eggs he cast aside; there was a tiny pin-hole through the shell. The others he ate with his usual composure. As he raised a cup of water to his lips the Brahoe, who had watched him with amazement, suddenly stretched out his hand in warning.

"Wait! it is poisoned," he whispered. "I will bring you more."

Swiftly he glided away and presently returned with a fresh bowl of clear water.

The physician drank without hesitation.

"You may go," said he, setting down the bowl.

"Master," said the man, "be warned. You are surrounded by dangers. But you are brave, and I am your servant henceforth. Eat hereafter only the food I bring you."

The Persian nodded and gave the Brahoe a smile. Still the man hesitated, peering cautiously about as if suspecting listeners. Finally he came nearer and said in a low voice:

"I do not know all; your foes are cunning and powerful. But the old khan is not to live the seven days. And life is lightly esteemed in Mekran—if it stands in the way of a purpose. Do not sleep tonight."

"I never sleep," returned the Persian, looking upon the man curiously.

Indeed, the critical condition of Burah Khan seemed to require his constant attention. The strange physician watched the silent form carefully throughout the night, and only once noted a slight movement of the draperies that guarded the entrance to the chamber.

At daybreak he drew the curtains of the windows to let in the light, and turned about in time to dash his heel upon the head of a small but venomous serpent that was poised to strike him with its fangs. Someone had placed it in the room during the night—a messenger of death to either the Khan or his physician, it mattered little which.

The Persian stared at the writhing snake a moment and made a gesture of impatience.

"It is only the fourth day," he muttered. "I wonder where Dirrag is."

An hour later the woman brought in his breakfast.

"Where is the Brahoe?" he demanded, sharply.

"He was found dead this morning," said the woman, shuddering. "Some enemy, it seems, strangled him while he slept."

The frown upon the Persian's brow was so fierce that the woman slipped away in terror.

"It is only the fourth day," he growled again, between set teeth; "but the Khan shall live until the seventh day—unless Dirrag comes before. I have sworn it, and, by Allah, I will keep my oath!"

VI

THE MAN OF DESTINY

A young man paced with nervous strides an open gallery of the ancient monastery of Mehmet, set high upon the mountain peak of Takkatu. He was tall and slender, his face worn thin by fasting and endless vigils, his shoulders stooping, his hands so emaciated that the fingers resembled eagles' talons. His forehead was high and protruding; his eyes bright and glistening; but the lower part of his face, from the small, delicate nose to the receding chin, indicated a weak and vacillating character.

Prone upon a narrow divan against the wall reclined another man, also young but of stalwart, rugged frame and with calm and well-fashioned features. His pose was absolutely without motion: not even a muscle twitched. The dark lashes lay over his closed eyes without a tremor.

Both wore the loose yellow gowns and high turbans of the Sunnite novitiates, but the one who paced the marble tiles had a band of white around his flowing sleeve—an indication of his superior degree.

Through the open peristyle came spicy breezes from near-by Araby. The sun cast intense shadows; a mighty stillness enveloped the monastery, as if the world slept.

The two novitiates were not alone. On a stone bench near the outer arches was seated an aged priest, clothed all in pure white, whose set face and hard, unseeing eyes indicated him wholly oblivious of his surroundings. Neither the young men seemed to consider his presence, although from time to time the nervous pacer would cast a swift glance in his direction.

Suddenly the latter paused before the divan.

"Give me your counsel, Hafiz!" said he, addressing the prostrate form. "Tell me what I must do."

The man upon the divan moved and sat up, regarding the other gravely with clear grey eyes.

"Well?" said he.

"Must I submit to it?" asked the other, eagerly. "Has my father the right to make this unreasonable, unjust, shameful demand?"

Hafiz nodded.

"After all these years of study and research," continued the slender brother, with a passionate gesture, "after a life devoted to religious concentration, to the worship of Allah and His divine manifestations on earth; after delving far into the inner mysteries of the Faith and seeing the day approach when I shall become of the Imaum—after this holy life in this holy temple must I be dragged into the coarse, material world again? Bah! it is outrageous—impossible!"

"Yet imperative," added the man on the divan.

His companion had resumed his agitated walk, but suddenly paused again and cast a frightened look at the placid countenance turned upon him. Then the frown faded from his own brow; his eyes softened and he said, gently:

"Forgive me, dear Hafiz! I am beside myself with grief. Tell me what I must do!"

"They have sent for you?" asked Hafiz.

"Yes. My father, the Khan, who has forgotten me since I came here, a little child, is now dying, and he commands my presence that I may succeed him as ruler of the tribes of Mekran."

"Have you known e'er this that you were Prince of Mekran?"

"Not till this hour, when our beloved mufti revealed to me the tidings."

"But *he* knew it?" said Hafiz, with a glance toward the entranced priest by the arch.

"Yes; he knew it, but preserved the knowledge. It seems there was reason for this. My father's house has powerful enemies, who would gladly have murdered his heir in childhood. So that no one but the Khan and his trusted vizier knew where I have been hidden all these years. And I—I have grown to manhood with the belief that I might devote my life to religion; yet now, when my soul craves peace and that exaltation which is accorded only to Allah's chosen servants, I am rudely summoned to a life of worldly turmoil, to take part in endless political intrigues and brutal warfares—all of which my spirit loathes."

"'Tis fate, Ahmed," said the other, thoughtfully, "and to be borne with the resignation our creed teaches. You are of royal birth, of an ancient line of heaven-born rulers, and you must fulfill your destiny."

"Ah, now you have given me my argument," retorted Ahmed, with a quick smile. "I am not of an ancient line of heaven-born rulers. We are usurpers."

"Yes?"

"Yes. My grandfather, according to the tale I have just heard, was a younger brother of the reigning khan, whom he ruthlessly slew and supplanted. By terrible and bloody wars my grandsire Keedar conquered the tribes that were faithful to his brother's son, and forced them to acknowledge and obey him. A fierce man was Keedar Khan, and always more hated than loved. But before he died all Baluchistan rendered him homage, and his son, my father, proved as stern and warlike as his sire. For thirty years he has ruled with an iron hand, and is today known to the world as the Lion of Mekran."

"Yet he is dying?"

"He is dying; and he sends for me, his only child, that I may be acknowledged his successor before the assembled sirdars of the nation."

"You must go."

"Think what that means!"

"You will be khan."

"Ruler of a nation of disaffected tribes, half of whom are eager to return to the allegiance of their rightful sovereign and who have only been held in subjection through two generations by the might of an iron will and the right of a gleaming sword."

"Who is this rightful sovereign you mention?"

"My cousin Kasam, whom I have never heard of until this day. He has been educated in foreign lands, I am told, to guard him from my father—as I have been reared in this holy place to prevent my being killed by the enemies of our house."

"And you would reject a throne—a throne bequeathed you by a warrior sire—because there is a pretender to the place?" asked Hafiz, with calm features but sparkling eyes. "It was by the sword the first royal family reigned in Mekran; it is by the sword your family reigns. Your duty is to your own kin. Let your strong arm maintain the power your ancestors have won and established!"

Ahmed shrank from the flashing eyes of his friend and spread out his palms with a deprecating gesture.

"I am no warrior, Hafiz. I am an humble servant of Allah. In a month I shall be Imaum!"

Hafiz gazed upon the slender, shrinking form of the heir of Mekran with earnestness. Truly it seemed unwise to urge the gentle devotee to abandon the monastery for the intrigue of a palace. He sighed, this stalwart, broad-shouldered monk of Takkatu, and reclined anew upon the divan.

"I wish," he said, regretfully, "I had been born the son of your father."

For a time Ahmed resumed his fretful pacing of the gallery, and no sound but his footsteps fell upon the ears of the three. The aged priest still sat, immobile, at his post, and the tall monk reclined as motionless upon his divan.

At times Ahmed would pause and wring his thin hands, murmuring: "I cannot! I cannot leave this holy place. In a month I shall be Imaum—a chosen comrade of the Prophet!"

A bell, low-toned and sweet, chimed from a neighboring spire. At the summons the priest stirred and turned himself to the east, the involuntary action being imitated by the younger men. Then all three cast themselves prone upon the marble floor, while a distant voice came softly but clearly to their ears, chanting the words: *"Allah is great. There no god but Allah. Come ye to prayer. Come ye to security!"*

As the tones faded away Ahmed groaned, repeating the words: "Security! come ye to security! O Allah, help me!"

But the others remained silent and motionless for a protracted time, and even Ahmed ceased his muttering and succumbed to the impressiveness of the mid-day prayer.

Finally the priest arose and made a sign.

"Retire, my son," said he to Ahmed, "and compose thy soul to peace. Allah has shown me the way."

The young man gave a start, his features suffused with a glow of delight, his eyes sparkling joyfully. Then he bowed low before the mufti and left the gallery with steady steps.

Hafiz remained, curiously regarding the aged priest, whose lean face now wore a look of keen intelligence. He came close to the stalwart novitiate and fixed upon him a piercing gaze.

"Allah is above all," he said, "and Mahomet is the Prophet of Allah. Next to them stands the Khan—the Protector of the Faith."

"It is true," answered Hafiz.

"Prince Kasam has been educated in London. His faith, be he still true to Mahomet, is lax. For the glory of Allah and the protection of our order, a true believer must rule at Mekran. The son of Burah Khan must sit in his father's place."

"It is true," said Hafiz, again.

"Yet our beloved brother, Ahmed, is about to become of the Imaum. His soul is with Allah. His hand is not fitted to grasp the sword. Shall we rob the Faith of its most earnest devotee?"

The calm grey eyes and the glittering black ones met, and a wave of intelligence vibrated between them.

Hafiz made no reply in words, and the priest paused in deep thought. At length he continued.

"For seven years, my brother, you have been one of us, and we have learned to love you. You came among us fresh from a life tragedy. You suffered. Allah comforted you, and within our walls you found peace. The sun and wind kissed your cheeks and turned them brown; your strength increased. The purity of your soul was grateful to the Prophet, and he granted you knowledge and understanding. But you were not destined to become a priest, my Hafiz. Allah has chosen you for a more worldly life, wherein you may yet render Him service by becoming a bulwark of the Faith!"

A smile softened the stern chin of the novitiate and lent his face a rare sweetness.

"I understand, O Mufti," he answered; but there was a thrill in his voice he could not repress.

The priest clapped his hands and an attendant entered.

"Send to me Dirrag the messenger," he commanded.

No word was spoken on the gallery until the son of Ugg appeared.

Dirrag was still white with the dust of his swift ride across the desert. He came in with a swinging stride, glanced with a momentary hesitation from one to the other of the two men, and then knelt humbly before Hafiz.

"My lord," said he, "your father commands your presence in Mekran. We must ride fast if you are to find him still alive."

"In an hour," answered the priest, calmly, "Prince Ahmed will be in the saddle. I commend to your wisdom and loyalty, good Dirrag, the safety of the heir to the throne of Mekran."

VII

DIRRAG

When Burah Khan picked Dirrag of the tribe of Ugg as his messenger to the monastery of Takkatu, he knew his man.

Dirrag was brother to the sirdar of his tribe, and the tribe of Ugg was Burah Khan's tribe, prominent above all others for having furnished two great rulers to the nation: Keedar the Great and his warrior son the Lion of Mekran. Well might the tribe of Ugg be proud, and well might Dirrag be faithful to his own kin.

The messenger was thin and wiry; he was not a tall man, but neither was Burah Khan, for that matter. Dirrag wore a black, thick beard that covered nearly his entire face. His eyes, as they glinted through the thicket of whisker, were keen as a ferret's. One of his ears had been sliced away by a cimeter; his left hand had but one finger and the thumb remaining; his body was seared with scars on almost every inch of its compact surface. Dirrag was no longer ornamental—if he had ever possessed that quality— but he was an exceedingly useful man in a skirmish and had fought for years beside Burah himself. They knew each other.

When Dirrag mounted his mare at the castle gates he did not hesitate as to his direction, but sped away toward the mountains. An ordinary messenger would have headed due east, so as to pass around the mountain range and reach by easy ascent the height of Takkatu. But the strange physician had told him Prince Ahmed must be at his father's side in six days, and Dirrag had looked into the man's eyes. He knew that much depended upon his promptness in fulfilling his mission, and so he rode, straight as the bird flies, toward Mount Takkatu.

And he rode swiftly, hour after hour, till shadows crept over the land and night fell. He dipped the mare's nose into two streams between then and daybreak, but paused only during those moments. At sunrise he dashed up to an enclosure, drew the bridle from his panting mare, threw it over the head of a snow-white stallion corralled near by, sprang astride the fresh animal and was off like the wind.

A Baluch came from a stone hut, watched the cloud of dust that marked Dirrag's flight and then calmly proceeded to tend and groom the weary mare the messenger had discarded.

"Oh, ho!" he muttered, "old Burah has the death-sickness at last, and the young prince is sent for. May Allah rest my master's black and scoundrelly soul!"

He had tended the relay for years, waiting for this hour.

Dirrag reached the monastery in the middle of the third day after leaving Mekran. He was obliged to curb his impatience for four tedious hours before the return journey could be begun. But the messenger was well ahead of his time, and provided Prince Ahmed proved a good rider would see Mekran again before the six days allotted him had sped.

There were good horses at the ancient monastery of Mehmet. No more famous stable existed in all Baluchistan. Dirrag glanced with pride at their mounts as he rode away beside his kinsman the prince. Also he noted with satisfaction the firm and graceful seat of his companion and his evident mastery of the splendid bay stallion he bestrode.

Therefore the warrior smiled grimly and tossed his head.

"Six days!" he muttered. "It is too many by one."

A long, swift stride the slender bays struck, and they maintained it hour after hour without seeming to tire. Dirrag was no chatterer, and the son of the Lion of Mekran, whom the tribesman regarded admiringly from time to time from the corner of his eye, seemed liable to prove equally reticent.

The warrior had never seen his master's son before, and had shared a common misgiving with the Baluchi concerning the monastery-bred prince. But his doubts were more than half relieved by his first view of the athletic form and steady poise of his kinsman. If the priests had not spoiled him—But, there! time would show. At present it was enough that the heir could ride.

Another day arrived before Dirrag was called upon to answer a single question. In the cool hour just before the sun arose, as they slowly rode up an incline, resting the horses for the long canter down hill, the prince asked:

"In what condition did you leave Burah Khan?"

"Your father, my prince, was near his end," he replied, slowly. "His illness has been long and tedious, and the Persian physician who arrived from Kelat gave him barely seven days to live. This is the fourth day."

"And when shall we reach Mekran?"

"On the morning of the sixth day—with the blessing of Allah."

The younger man pondered the matter long. Then he said:

"Who recommended the Persian? Were there no physicians in Mekran?"

"Burah beheaded his own physician three weeks ago. He has executed, altogether, five men of medicine since this illness came upon him. The others have fled or are in hiding. As for the Persian, I am told Agahr the Vizier would have prevented his coming; but Melka of our tribe, who rules the khan's harem, rode fast to Kelat, and the Persian came."

"Agahr. Is he not our cousin?"

"Your uncle, lord, thrice removed. He is own cousin to Kasam the Pretender."

Another period of silence, finally broken by questions as calmly and indifferently put.

"This Kasam the Pretender. Is he popular in Mekran?"

"They do not know him, anymore than they know yourself. He has lived in a far country since boyhood, and is said to be still there."

"But he has friends—partisans?"

Dirrag hitched uneasily in his seat.

"There are some, even yet, who deny the right of a son of Ugg to rule. Old Keedar did not strike softly, and the sword of Burah was ever long and sharp. You will have enemies, my master, when you are khan."

"Open enemies?"

"And secret ones. The open enemies you need not fear."

At noon they entered the Gedrusian Desert, the uplands being all behind them.

There is little danger in this tract of waste land to those familiar with it. Numerous pools and oases sustain the traveller of experience. Dirrag knew every inch of the desert, and as their present route was across but one corner of it he entered fearlessly.

Night had fallen and the moon and stars were out when they halted the weary horses beside a pool. Ahmed dismounted and had knelt beside the water to drink when Dirrag suddenly grasped his shoulder and threw him forcibly backward. He arose slowly, rearranged his burnous and cast an enquiring look at his companion.

"The pool is poisoned," said Dirrag.

Bending over, he pointed to the bottom of the shallow water, where the moon shone on several slender twigs that were covered with a pale green bark.

"It is from the shushalla—the snake-tree," he said, gruffly. "A drop of this water will bring instant death. This is very annoying. Our pools are never poisoned without a purpose, my master. Perhaps we are watched."

"I saw a rider against the horizon, as we came up," replied Ahmed.

He stretched his muscular arms, yawned with weariness and lay down upon the sand, instantly becoming motionless. It was a trick of relaxation he had learned at the Sunnite monastery.

Dirrag looked at him approvingly. The novitiate Hafiz had cast aside his yellow robes with his monastic name, and now wore the simple dress of a Baluch tribesman, without ornament or jewel of any sort. The fold of his turban, however, proclaimed him a member of the tribe of Ugg, and the cimeter at his side—the gift of the wily priest of Mehmet—was a weapon of rare quality, its hilt sparkling with clustered gems. Dirrag, when he first saw it, had made humble obeisance to the cimeter.

The former recluse also bore a short spear, with the accompanying shield of hammered bronze, and these completed his equipment.

Dirrag, wondering vaguely if his young master knew how to handle his weapons, unsheathed his own blade and, squatting at the edge of the pool, impaled the green twigs, one after another, upon its point and drew them from the water. When all had been thus removed he buried the deadly branches deep in the desert sands, and then reclined beside his master. The horses sniffed eagerly at the pool, but would not drink until they were given permission.

Silence fell upon the group. When three hours had passed Dirrag arose, crept to the pool and dipped his finger in the water, tasting a drop warily. Then he leaned over and drank, somewhat sparingly, and laid himself down again, commending his soul to Allah.

In another hour he sprang up, alert and brisk, and touched Ahmed's shoulder.

"You may drink, master," said he. "The pool is cleansed."

Five minutes later, men and horses alike refreshed, they galloped away through the moonlight.

The fifth day dawned—the fifth according to Dirrag's calendar, which dated from the moment he had left Mekran. Ahmed had been in the saddle thirty-six hours, with brief periods of rest. Dirrag, man of iron though he was, began to show signs of fatigue. He was used to long riding, but now his eyelashes seemed lead and every stroke of his horse's hoofs sounded in his ears like the beat of a drum.

Soon after the sun arose they discovered a group of horsemen far across the desert, who seemed to be riding in the same direction they were. The horsemen were mere specks upon the sands, at first, but as the hours passed they grew larger.

"Travellers to Mekran," remarked Dirrag, calmly. "The sirdars have been assembled. Doubtless it is the party of some dignitary journeying to the death-bed of Burah Khan."

"How far distant is Mekran?" asked Ahmed.

"We shall reach it, Allah willing, by another daybreak," replied the warrior. "It will be the morning of the sixth day. The Persian gave me full six days. I shall save twelve hours, and twelve hours to a dying man is a long time."

There was an accent of pride in his voice. Agahr had said the journey would require seven days with fast riding. But Agahr was a townsman; how should he know how fast the men of Ugg can ride?

The group of horsemen drew nearer. At noon Dirrag could see them almost plainly enough to determine what tribe they belonged to—almost, but not quite. Shortly afterwards, however, they whirled and rode directly toward the two travellers, and then Dirrag straightened in his saddle, cast the sleep from his eyes and gave a low growl.

"They are of the Tribe of Raab—a wild and rebellious band that hates Burah and supports the cause of Kasam the Pretender."

"Why are they here?" asked Ahmed.

"To prevent our reaching Mekran I suppose. They do not want the sirdars and your father to publicly acknowledge you the successor to the throne."

"Well?"

"It was for the same reason the pool was poisoned. Treachery first; then the sword. Can you fight, my prince?"

"I can try," smiled Ahmed. "We are taught the arts of warfare in the monastery."

"You surprise me. I thought the priests passed their time in the worship of Allah."

"And in preparing to defend the Faith, good Dirrag. Yet I do not know how well I can wield a cimeter in actual combat. Naked steel differs from a wooden foil. And the men of Raab outnumber us."

"There are a dozen of them, at least. But you and I are of the tribe of Ugg. If we cannot win the fight we may at least honor our kinsmen by taking three lives to our one."

"It is worth the trial," returned Ahmed, cheerfully, and he drew the cimeter from its leathern sheath and eyed the blade curiously.

"The spear first, my lord," said Dirrag. "After that the sword play. These men of Raab are not skillful, but they are brave." And he proceeded to instruct Ahmed in the conduct of the coming encounter.

The horsemen were now so near that their shouts could be plainly heard. They were racing on at full speed, waving their spears in the air as they rode.

"See!" exclaimed Ahmed, after a glance over his shoulder. "We are being surrounded."

Dirrag looked and growled again; but there was a more cheerful note to his voice this time.

"A caravan!" he exclaimed. "They are yet far off, but they have dromedaries and are swiftly approaching. If we can escape the first attack of the assassins we may be rescued yet."

There was no time for further words. The fierce tribesmen of Raab were quickly upon them, and by a concerted movement Ahmed and Dirrag whirled their horses in opposite directions, separating as they dashed away over the sands. This was intended to cause the band to divide, a part following each fugitive. But, to Dirrag's annoyance, only two came after him, yelling and shaking their spears, indeed, but seeming not over anxious to engage him in combat, so long as he did not rejoin Ahmed.

It was upon the young heir of Mekran that most of the Raabites hurled themselves, circling around him at full gallop and watching a chance to thrust a spear into his back.

Ahmed recognized his peril. He cast his spear at one assailant, cleft another through turban and skull with his keen cimeter, and then, with a word to the gallant bay of Mehmet, he raised the horse high in the air and hurled it like a catapult at the foeman who chanced to be before him.

Even at the moment of impact the glittering blade whistled again through the air and the man of Raab sprawled with his horse in the desert sands, while Ahmed's steed broke through the circle of his foes and bounded away to rejoin Dirrag, who was so lost in admiration of his young master's prowess that he hardly looked to defend himself from his own assailants.

"Shall we fly?" asked Ahmed.

"It is useless," panted Dirrag, ranging his horse beside that of his master, so that it faced the opposite direction. "They can outrun us easily, for our steeds are weary. But a few more strokes like those, my prince, and the dogs will themselves take to their heels."

There was no indication of this at present, however. Again the enemy with fierce determination surrounded the two, and while each guarded the other's back they sat side by side and gave stroke for stroke with calm precision.

"Hold!" cried an eager voice, sounding above the melee.

The men of Raab, as if fearful of being robbed of their prey, made a sudden furious dash. At the same time a pistol shot rang out and the leader tumbled from his saddle. The Raabites were demoralized, and fell back. They had no fire-arms.

"Forbear, I command you!" said the same imperative voice. "I am Prince Kasam."

Yells of surprise and disappointment broke from the tribesmen. With a sudden impulse they wheeled and galloped swiftly over the desert, while the rescued men wearied and breathless, lowered their swords to gaze around them in surprise.

The caravan had come upon them unawares. Twenty stout Afghans rode back of the young prince who had interrupted the conflict, and behind these stood dromedaries upon whose ample backs were perched ladies in European dress and gentlemen composedly smoking cheroots.

"Well done, Kasam," cried Colonel Moore, approvingly, and the ladies waved their handkerchiefs.

Dirrag, who had dismounted to pull a spear-head from his horse's flank, scowled and shrank back so that the bay's body partly hid him. Ahmed, at the sound of English words, drew the folds of his burnous close about his face, so that only the grey eyes were left revealed; but he sat his horse quietly and gave the native salute.

"We thank Prince Kasam for our rescue," he said in the native tongue.

Kasam flushed and laughed good-naturedly.

"Keep my secret, friend," he returned. "I was, indeed, foolish to reveal my station to that rabble yonder. But they are men of Raab, from which tribe I am myself descended, and in the emergency it seemed the only way to compel their obedience."

The other bowed coldly and turned away to watch the Afghans rifling the bodies of the fallen.

"Bury those fellows in the sand," ordered Kasam, shivering as he looked at the stark forms. "Were they not of my tribe they should feed the jackals for so cowardly an attack. What was your quarrel, friend?" turning again to Ahmed.

The latter made no reply, waving a hand toward Dirrag. Whereat the warrior, despite his repugnance, forced himself to come forward and answer for his silent chief.

"We are of the tribe of Ugg," said he, briefly.

Kasam laughed.

"That is the usurper's tribe," said he; "the tribe of old Burah, who is either dying or dead at this moment. No wonder my kinsmen assailed you!"

Some of the ladies and gentlemen, who had understood nothing of this conversation, now rode forward with eager questions in English concerning the affray and those who had been slain. Bessie screamed at sight of the mound of sand that was being rapidly heaped over the victims, and Aunt Lucy declared she was about to faint and would fall off the camel. Dr. Warner, in well chosen words, denounced a country where such murderous assaults were possible, and the Colonel regretted they had not arrived in time to see more of the fight. Even Allison Moore displayed considerable interest in the incident, and condemned Kasam for interrupting what might have been "a very pretty scrap."

Meantime Ahmed, with muffled face, sat his horse as if turned to stone, and Dirrag scowled more and more at the gabble of the foreigners.

"Friend," said Kasam, mistaking the scarred warrior for the leader of the two, "we are riding to Mekran. If you travel our way you have permission to attach yourselves to my caravan. It will doubtless insure your safety."

To what extent Dirrag might have resented this implication that they were unable to protect themselves is uncertain, for an ungracious reply on his part to the kindly-meant invitation was interrupted by a recollection of the importance of his mission and the dangers that now menaced his young companion.

"Prince Kasam has our thanks," he muttered. "We journey to Mekran."

As the caravan started anew Janet Moore, who had remained quietly in the background, among the baggage-men and camel-drivers, rode slowly forward and joined the group of Americans. Whereupon Bessie laughingly reproached her for her timidity, and began chattering an unintelligible explanation of what had happened.

The men of Ugg silently joined the caravan. Neither they nor their horses seemed much the worse for the conflict, although Dirrag's animal had a gaping wound in the thigh that would soon become stiff and sore, and the warrior had himself added a scratch across the forehead to his collection of wounds.

"Your countrymen seem to regard life very lightly, Prince," said the Colonel, as they rode together near the front.

"Among themselves they have fought for centuries," answered Kasam. "Yet I am told that of late years, under Keedar and Burah Khan, these minor frays have been forbidden and the combatants, if caught, severely punished. But old Burah is as good as dead, now, and the squabbles of the tribesmen are likely to break out afresh until I have time to reorganize the government and pacify the country."

"Will you, too, be known as 'a fighting khan,' such as the 'Lion of Mekran?'" asked Bessie, looking upon the young man with admiring eyes.

"I hope not, indeed," he replied, laughing. "I shall try to instil European ideas into the heads of my stupid countrymen, and teach them the superiority of the Arts of Peace."

None noticed that Ahmed's horse had gradually forged ahead until he rode just behind the party of Americans.

"Isn't it queer," remarked Miss Warner, musingly, "that the future potentate of this big country is personally conducting us to his capital? It was really nice of you, Prince, to return with our passports. For a time we thought you had forsaken us, and Allison was bent on our retracing our steps and quitting the country."

Kasam glanced into Janet's grave face.

"You need not fear my deserting you," he said earnestly. "Indeed, had I remained in Mekran during these days of waiting for the Khan's death I should have gone wild with suspense, for there is nothing that can be done until Burah breathes his last breath. His physician, a stubborn Persian, promised him life for seven days."

"Suppose the Persian fails, and you are absent?" suggested the Colonel.

"If the Persian fails, so much the better," returned Kasam; "for then the monk-taught weakling son of Burah will not be acknowledged his successor, and the title of Khan reverts to me."

"But if the son arrives before his father's death?"

It was the doctor who asked this question.

"Then we revolt—I believe that is the plan—and drive every member of the tribe of Ugg from Mekran. But my cousin Ahmed cannot arrive before the seventh day, which is the day after tomorrow, and, according to my uncle Agahr, who is clever at intrigue, it will not be possible for Burah's son to arrive at all."

"Why not?" demanded the Colonel.

"Assassination, I suppose," suggested the doctor.

Kasam shrugged his shoulders.

"I do not ask my Uncle Agahr to explain these things. Ahmed is not to be assassinated, however; he promised me that. Otherwise, it matters little what prevents him from reaching his father's death-bed."

"What a splendid man that barbarian is!" whispered Bessie to Janet. The latter turned slowly in her seat and gave a start of surprise, for Ahmed rode just behind her. The look in the calm grey eyes seemed to thrill the girl strangely, for she swayed in her saddle and might have fallen had not the "barbarian" thrust out a strong arm and steadied her.

"What are you doing here?" cried Kasam, angrily, in the native Baluch. "Back to the rear, my man, where you belong!"

Ahmed bowed gravely and retreated to where Dirrag rode. Nor did he again venture near the front.

"How cross you were to that handsome fellow," said Bessie, pouting her pretty lips.

"Why, as for that, Miss Bessie," returned the Prince, "I happened to remember that I was indulging rather freely in political gossip; and while it is impossible that he should understand English, your handsome fellow is of the tribe of Ugg—our hereditary foes."

"If all the tribe of Ugg are like these two samples," remarked the doctor, "it may not be so easy to thrust them from your capital."

"They are not, I suppose. I do not remember to have seen so fine a specimen of manhood as the tall one among the natives before. What a pity that I know so little of my own country," continued the young man regretfully. "Did you notice how reverent my Afghans are toward that little, battle-scarred warrior we rescued? He may be some man of note—some mighty hero—for all I know. But doubtless he is a mere quarrelsome tribesman, beneath my notice. When I am khan I shall make it a point to study my people thoroughly, that I may better understand how to manage them."

At sundown they reached the edge of the desert and came to the fertile plains of Melin. Here camp was made and, wearied with the day's journey, the travellers made their repast and retired early to rest.

"Tomorrow night we shall sleep in Mekran," said Kasam. "I am sorry

I cannot invite you directly to the palace; but until old Burah dies I am as much a stranger in my own country as any of you. However, my Uncle Agahr will see that you are provided with comfortable quarters."

"Are there no inns in Mekran?" asked Allison.

"Inns are plentiful, but afford only the most primitive accommodations. We must house you in the dwelling of one of our adherents. There are many of these, I assure you, of rank and wealth. And now, I bid you goodnight, ladies. May Allah guard your rest."

At the door of their tent the doctor and Colonel Moore smoked a cigar before retiring.

"I am sorry," said the latter, in a low voice, "that in my ignorance of Baluchistan I permitted the girls and Aunt Lucy to accompany us."

"They've stood the trip pretty well, so far," replied the doctor, carelessly.

"Yes; but consider what a mess the country is in, politically. There's liable to be open warfare—perhaps a massacre—in a day or two, according to Kasam. And the girls may—"

"Oh, we'll keep the girls out of danger," declared the doctor. "I've no doubt they are as safe here as at home. I will acknowledge the country is more wild and uncivilized than I had dreamed, but we're on a matter of business, Colonel, and I flatter myself we have as good as accomplished our purpose already. Kasam is sure to grant us right of way for our railroad—when he is khan."

The Colonel smoked a while in silence.

"This young man," he remarked, at length, "seems to have little doubt of the success of his cause. Yet from all I have picked up since we drew near to Baluchistan, that terrible Burah Khan who is dying is absolute master of the situation. And his son—"

"His son is a priest-ridden devotee of Mahomet, who knows better how to pray than to rule a turbulent nation. Don't worry about Kasam, my dear Colonel. He's sure to win out. And if he doesn't—"

The doctor smiled cynically.

"What then?"

"Why, if he doesn't," retorted the doctor, tossing away his cigar and rising to retire, "the priest-bred weakling—is his name Ahmed?—will be just the sort of ruler the Metropolitan Construction Company loves to deal with. However the cat jumps we are sure to have the railway; so let's go to bed."

Just before daybreak the leader of the Afghans came to Kasam's tent and awoke him.

"The men of Ugg are gone," said he.

"Never mind," returned the Prince, sitting up to yawn. "When did they go?"

"Early last evening; soon after we made camp. They stole away unobserved."

"It doesn't matter in the least," said Kasam.

"Except that they have taken your Excellency's black stallion, and left in its place the wounded bay, which is too stiff to travel."

"Why, that was base ingratitude," said the young man, with unconcern. "I must punish those fellows, if ever I see them again. But it is only a day's journey to Mekran. I'll ride a dromedary, good captain; and, by the way, let us make an early start."

But at the same moment that Prince Kasam's camp was awakening to activity Ahmed and Dirrag, after a night's hard gallop, rode through the marble gates of Mekran.

It was the morning of the sixth day.

VIII

A Woman's Way

A nd now," the vizier had said to his daughter on the evening of the fourth day, "let us rest content. The sirdar of the tribe of Raab—our faithful ally Zarig—has sent a force to patrol the desert trails over which Dirrag must pass with Ahmed on his return to Mekran. Zarig has sworn that the son of Burah shall never reach here by the seventh day."

"That is good," answered Maie, thoughtfully. "But it is not enough."

Agahr threw out his palms with an impulsive gesture.

"What would you have?" he asked, impatiently. "I have suborned every servant in the palace; I have followed every plan you have suggested; intrigue and cunning each moment battle for our great object."

"Yet the Persian sits beside Burah Khan and baffles our every plot," replied the girl. "I will go to him myself, my father."

"You! Impossible."

"No one shall ever know but yourself, and you will guard my secret. But see the Persian I must. Despite his pretended loyalty he is a mere man—and surely there is a way to influence any man that lives."

An hour later Agahr secretly introduced Maie into the palace, and while he himself guarded the passage leading to the chamber of Burah the girl boldly pushed aside the draperies at the entrance and confronted the physician.

The Persian was standing beside the couch as she entered, and after a glance at his visitor he quietly drew a silken coverlet over the still form and advanced to where the girl stood awaiting him.

"I am the daughter of the vizier," she said, softly.

"You are welcome," declared the Persian; but he passed one hand over his forehead as he spoke, and his voice sounded weary and discouraged.

Maie threw back her veil and smiled, while the physician, leaning upon the low table that bore the shaded lamp, gazed wonderingly at the beautiful face revealed.

"May I rest myself?" she asked, in her sweet voice, and without awaiting permission she passed between the table and Burah's couch and sank gracefully upon a low divan.

The Persian hesitated an instant, and cast an uneasy glance at his patient. Then he seated himself beside the table and bowed.

"It is the same old tale, I suppose?" he said, enquiringly. "You do not wish the Khan to live to acknowledge his son?"

The girl gave a little laugh.

"It is very pleasant to find you both frank and comprehensive," she returned, "for now many useless words may be spared. Tell me, Persian, why you insist upon interfering with our plans to depose the sons of Ugg and restore the throne to the former rulers of Baluchistan? What is it to you, a stranger, whether Burah Khan dies tonight—this very moment—or lives to acknowledge his son two days hence?"

"Only this," he answered quietly. "I have given my word."

"Do you fear for your reputation as a skillful physician? Elai! You have already accomplished wonders enough to make you famous. Had you not arrived in Mekran, Burah Khan long since would have passed away."

"It was a draught of my own invention," said the man, musingly. "I am anxious to test its powers. If it will hold Death at bay for seven days I shall have solved an important problem in medical science."

"But why is it necessary to test your draught on the Khan of Baluchistan? There may be thousands of similar cases wherein the matter of life and death is unimportant. Perhaps, in spite of your great fame, you lack money. See!"

With a quick gesture she arose and approached the table, emptying upon its spread the contents of a chamois bag. Before the physician's eyes sparkled a score of exquisite gems—diamonds, rubies, sapphires and emeralds of enormous value.

He gave them but a glance and looked into the girl's eyes. They sparkled as brilliantly as the jewels, but were equally mystifying. What she read in his own eyes is uncertain, but a moment later she sank at his feet and clasped his knees in her rounded arms.

"For the cause of science," she murmured, looking up into his face with a ravishing smile, "I will gladly promise the great physician ten gems, equally as flawless and pure, for everyone now before him! It is a rare treasure, my Persian. All I ask in return is permission to attend the Khan until morning."

His brow flushed, but he did not withdraw his gaze from her dark eyes.

"Ah, do not refuse me," she pleaded, resting her head against him so that the fragrance of her hair saluted his nostrils like an enchanting perfume. "It is so little for you to do, when you may ask so much in return!" Her bosom heaved with emotion and pressed against his knee. "You shall have a palace of your own, my friend, here in Mekran, where you may woo Science at your will and command a thousand slaves to do your bidding. Are we not playing for a throne? And who shall have greater power than the man that enables the new khan to sit therein and rule a kingdom? I am the daughter of the vizier, my Persian, and hereafter no physician but you shall attend me."

She nestled closer, with a little sigh of content that seemed to indicate the battle was won to their mutual satisfaction, and for a moment both maintained the pose, silent and motionless.

Suddenly the physician stood up, freeing himself from the girl's embrace. With an abrupt motion he swept the glittering gems into the little bag and tossed it at the girl's feet. Then, with folded arms, he stood looking down at where she still crouched by the empty chair, her lovely features convulsed with a passion terrible to witness.

But the mood quickly passed. Her face cleared. She raised her hand and rearranged the disordered masses of her hair, laughing the while in low tones and lifting her eyes unabashed to the man who had repulsed her.

The Persian shuddered.

Slowly rising to her feet she made him a mocking bow and said, jestingly:

"The chisel must indeed be dull that can carve no emblem on the marble. No man, believe me, is incorruptible; I have failed merely because I overestimated my own powers. Well, I will go."

She looked around for her cloak. It lay over the divan, and she passed the Persian as if to get it. But in the act of picking it up she paused, straightened, and in two bounds stood beside the couch of the unconscious khan. A dagger flashed, and once—twice—thrice she plunged it deep into the bosom of the form hidden by the silken coverlet. Then she turned with a laugh of triumph toward the physician, the dagger still clasped in her jewelled fingers.

The Persian smiled.

Without a word he walked to the couch, and as she shrank aside he seized the coverlet and thrust it back, revealing nothing more than a mass of bolsters and cushions cleverly placed to outline the form of a man.

The girl, rigid and staring, turned her eyes from the couch to the physician.

"Where is he?" she whispered.

He took her wrist, fearless of the dagger she still held, and led her to an alcove. Throwing back the curtains he allowed her to gaze upon the still form of Burah Khan, lying peacefully beside a window through which the moon's rays flooded the small apartment with mellow light.

Maie made no attempt to escape the grasp upon her wrist. She permitted the man to lead her back to the larger room, where he wrapped the cloak around her shoulders and placed the bag of jewels in her hand.

A moment later she rejoined the vizier in the passage.

"Well?" he enquired, anxiously.

"We must pin our faith to the men of Raab," she replied, between her set teeth. "The Persian is not human—he is a fiend!"

IX

The Sixth Day

Dirrag led his master straight to the royal palace, reaching it just as the first rays of the sun fell upon the city. As he arrived unexpectedly, there was none to receive him except a few sleepy servants and the sirdars of the tribes of Mem and Agot, who shared the watch over the chamber of the khan. These, being loyal to the reigning house, were overjoyed at the speedy and safe return of the messenger, and cast curious glances at his tall companion.

But Dirrag knew where his duty lay and did not linger an instant. He pressed on to the khan's own chamber, and entered without announcement, followed closely by Ahmed.

The Persian stood by an open window, engaged in rolling a cigarette. He paused, motionless, as he saw Dirrag. His eye lighted with satisfaction, and he drew a sigh of relief.

"Back already!" he said, pleasantly.

"As you see," answered Dirrag, with pride. "It is the morning of the sixth day, and I have saved twelve hours from my allotted time. And here is Prince Ahmed, the son of Burah Khan, and heir to the Lion of Mekran—safe and sound, although nearly as weary as I am myself."

A long speech for Dirrag, but warranted by the marvelous ride he had so successfully accomplished.

The Persian seemed not to hear it. He was staring fixedly at the tall form of the Prince.

"You!" he gasped, as if a great surprise overwhelmed him.

Ahmed, with wide eyes reading the other through and through, and seemingly filled with equal astonishment, answered steadily and briefly:

"I am the man."

"I have searched for you throughout the East," said the Physician, recovering in a degree his composure. "And now—"

"Now you have found me," returned Ahmed, smiling upon the other.

The two men clasped hands, and Dirrag, uneasily regarding the amazing thing, shifted his booted feet back and forth with a child's nervousness.

"You the son of Burah Khan!" exclaimed one.

"You the famed physician of Persia!" said the other.

But Dirrag did not understand. They spoke a queer language unknown to him.

Presently, however, the physician noted his distress and drew away from the Prince, saying in the Baluch tongue:

"My lord the Prince Ahmed is welcome. It is fortunate for us all that he has arrived safely."

"And in time, I hope?" enquired Ahmed, eagerly. "How is my—how is Burah Khan's health?"

The Persian gave a little laugh, sat down, and proceeded to light his cigarette.

"Burah Khan is dead," said he.

"Dead!"

The physician nodded, blowing a cloud of smoke from his nostrils. Dirrag gave a groan and sank limply into a chair. Ahmed, with a swift glance into the Persian's face, merely frowned and stood at attention, as if waiting to hear more.

"It is doubtless a great misfortune," continued the physician, speaking in a leisurely tone, "and I have been in a desperate quandary, having no one in all the throng surrounding the late khan in whom I dared confide. The vizier is a traitor, and at the head of a formidable conspiracy. The sirdars, with one exception, are faithful; but they are warriors, and not fitted to counsel in so delicate a matter as this. So I have watched beside the khan's dead body for two days and two nights, and none save myself knew he had ceased to breathe."

"But, elai! did you not promise—" began Dirrag, in a boisterous tone.

"I did," interrupted the other, coolly. "I promised Burah Khan should live seven days—even while I saw the death-damp upon his brow. For I read the vizier clearly, and suspected there was a conspiracy to supplant the dying man's son. It mattered nothing to me except that it gave me pleasure to try to defeat the plot old Burah was himself unable to foil. Moreover, I had faith in a peculiar powder that has been known to hold life within a body for many days. It seemed the game was worth the candle, did it not? And the old khan, to my great satisfaction, did manage to live for four days of the six required by Dirrag to make the journey to Takkatu and back. Then he died without awakening."

"It is terrible," said Dirrag, wiping the sweat from his brow.

"Not so," returned the physician, with an odd smile. "A man has ample time to think when he sits by a dead body. We three are the sole owners of the secret. Well? Shall we ring down the curtain, or go on with the play?"

"The play!" repeated Dirrag, vacantly.

"It is all a play, my friend," said the Persian, reassuringly, "and we, living or dead, are expected to assume our characters to the end. So, if an honest man is sometimes called upon to enact the part of a villain, it is not greatly to his discredit."

Ahmed stepped close to the physician and his grey eyes gazed full into the other's brown ones.

"If I become khan," said he, "it will be due to your friendly offices."

"I acknowledge it," the physician replied.

"If I become khan," persisted Ahmed, in the same level tone, "no man on earth shall dictate my acts or cripple my power."

The Persian smiled, indulgently.

"I will acknowledge that, also," said he.

"Then," continued the Prince, throwing himself upon a chair, "let the play go on!"

GREAT WAS THE EXCITEMENT IN Mekran when the news flew from palace to town that Dirrag had returned, bringing with him the son of the dying khan. Maie heard it from the mouth of a slave, and after one reproachful glance at her father sat silent and still as a graven image, while the vizier, with pallid face and a great fear at his heart, hastened away to the palace.

The men of Mem and Agot guarded the gateway and jeered openly at Agahr as he hurried through. Within the courtyard were assembled the sirdars and chiefs of all the fighting tribes of Baluchi, waiting in grim silence for the drama about to be enacted. They saluted the vizier.

Agahr started to ascend the stairway leading to the gallery that gave entrance to the khan's chamber; but a row of hard-featured men of Ugg forced him back. No one could be admitted until the Persian physician gave the order. He was preparing his patient for the ceremony.

"But I am the Khan's vizier!" protested the old man, trembling despite his effort at command.

A rugged warrior faced him and bowed low.

"In all else, master, your word is law," said he, courteously. "But in the chamber of death the physician rules supreme—by the grace of Allah and the will of His Highness the Khan."

Agahr turned and waited with the others in silence.

It was not long. A tall Arab slave, known as a favorite attendant of the Lion of Mekran, appeared upon the stairs and called aloud:

"Burah Khan, son of Keedar the Great, Headsman of the Nine Tribes of Baluchi and Defender of the Faith, commands the Sirdars of the Nation and the officers of his household to attend him!"

They obeyed at once, fully conscious of the mighty import of the message. The sirdars came first, followed by Agahr and the civil officers and then a long train of household retainers of lesser rank— all proceeding with dignified steps up the marble stairway, along the gallery, and so into the spacious chamber of the Khan.

The Arab slave, acting as major-domo, ranged them in the order of their rank, facing the curtained alcove in which lay the body of their ruler.

Then, as silence fell upon the throng, the curtains were drawn and those assembled gazed upon an impressive scene.

Upon a couch covered with costly furs reclined the Khan, his sunken features dimly outlined in the soft light and the jewelled stars upon his breast glinting darkly as his bosom rose and fell. Over him bent the strange physician, administering from a golden cup the draught which it was understood would restore the sick man to intelligence for a brief period. But after a glance at this tableau all eyes were turned to the upright form of a young man standing with folded arms at the head of the couch. He was clad in a magnificent robe of purple satin richly embroidered with pearls, and by his side hung the famous cimeter known to every sirdar as the sword of Keedar Khan, and which had been entrusted by Burah to the priests of the monastery for safe keeping until Prince Ahmed should be called to Mekran.

There was something in the majestic presence of the heir, his haughty bearing and the look of pride in the calm grey eyes that wandered from one to another of the faces confronting him, that sent a thrill through all the assemblage. To some that thrill meant elation, to some fear; but to all it brought a subtle recognition of the fact that here was the heritage of power, that the son of Burah and grandson of Keedar was a man to be promptly obeyed.

The physician, passing an arm under the sick man's head, supported him to a sitting position, and Burah Khan, after taking his son's right hand in his own, began speaking to his people slowly and in low, halting accents.

"Here—is Prince—Ahmed, my son and rightful—heir. I, Burah

Khan, standing—in the shadow of—death, do acknowledge him to be my—successor—to the throne of Mekran. Sirdars of the—Nine—Mighty Tribes of the—Baluchi, do ye, also, acknowledge him—to be your—Khan and Master—when I am gone?"

So still was the throng that every word of the faltering voice was distinctly heard. As it ceased the nine sirdars drew their swords and cast them at Ahmed's feet, crying aloud:

"We acknowledge Ahmed to be our Khan, when Allah claims his sire, Burah Khan."

Answering the shout was a sob and a sudden fall. The spectators drew aside with significant looks as slaves carried the fainting vizier from the chamber. Then all eyes turned again to the alcove.

Burah lay back upon his couch with closed eyes, and Ahmed knelt beside him.

The physician bent over and placed an ear above the old man's heart. Then he stood erect and signed to the Arab to draw the curtain.

"Burah Khan is dead," said he, solemnly. "May Allah and the Prophet grant him peace!"

The curtain fell, and very humbly and reverently the assembled people bowed their heads and crept from the chamber of death.

X

AHMED KHAN

B ehold the walls of Mekran!" said Kasam proudly.

They had been riding all afternoon through a beautiful and fertile valley, rich with fields of waving grain, tracts of vegetables, vineyards and orchards, all tended by the Kendars, Brahoes and Melinos, for the warlike Baluchi were too dignified to till the soil. It was from this valley that the city of Mekran derived its main sustenance and support, and now, as they mounted a little eminence, the city itself came into view—a huge, whitewashed stone wall above which peeped the roofs of many dwellings, mosques and palaces.

"The palace of the khan," said Kasam, "is near the center, beside the famous bubbling pools of Mekran. You may tell it by the high towers and minarets. It is all built of marble and its gardens are more beautiful than any in Europe."

"You may well be proud of this great city, which you are so soon to rule," observed Bessie, instantly connecting the prince with the place of his nativity. "It is one of the prettiest sights I have ever seen."

"We must make this an important depot for the new railway," said the Colonel, with something like enthusiasm. "The whole world will come to see Mekran when the journey can be made in Pullmans."

But as they drew nearer and the sun sank toward the horizon Mekran lost much of its beauty. The whitewash of the great wall was seen to be grimy and stained in many places, and the roofs above it showed considerable discoloration by the weather. It was an old city, and had long since lost the freshness of youth. Indeed, Allison took occasion to denounce, with some contempt, a place which seemed "nearly as filthy as the people of this beastly country themselves," and Kasam flushed slightly with a realization that neither Mekran nor his people could be counted quite immaculate.

Beneath the setting sun, however, the spires and domes glowed golden red, and even the young engineer ceased reviling the place they had come so far from civilization to visit.

At dusk the caravan entered at the North Gate, and Kasam called attention to the thickness of the wall as they rode through, and to the picturesque watch-tower perched above the gate. Then, coming into the light of the inner city he gave a start of surprise, for lining the sides of the narrow street were solid ranks of Baluchi warriors, both mounted and on foot, who stood so silently in their places that their presence was all unsuspected until the Prince came full upon them. Hesitating, he reigned in his horse, and at that moment the iron gates fell with a clang behind the last of his cavalcade.

"You are going to have a reception, Prince," remarked Dr. Warner, who rode near the guide.

Kasam muttered a curse and urged forward his horse. The Baluchi instantly closed their ranks, surrounding him with a solid phalanx.

"Welcome to Mekran, my lord," said a voice, and Kasam turned to find the warrior he had rescued in the desert riding at his stirrup. There was no mistaking Dirrag. The fresh scratch upon his brow marked his seared face with a streak of livid red.

"His Highness the Khan has requested your presence at the palace," continued the warrior, in respectful tones.

"Me?" asked the young man, startled.

"You are Prince Kasam, I believe."

"Ah, I begin to understand. You have betrayed me as a fitting return for having saved your life. It was to be expected in a man of Ugg. But why does old Burah demand my presence? Am I a prisoner?"

"Burah Khan is in Paradise," said Dirrag, gravely.

"Dead! . . . And his son?"

"Now rules as Ahmed Khan."

Kasam's bronzed features drew tense. He became silent.

As they turned a corner he noticed they had become detached from the others of his party and were now alone.

"Where are my companions?" he enquired, with anxiety. "I am guiding a party of foreigners, who are strange to Mekran."

"They will be safely cared for," answered Dirrag, reassuringly.

"And my Afghans?"

"They also. The Khan has provided for all."

The answers were far from satisfactory, but Kasam had perils of his own to confront, and dismissed his American friends from his thoughts with the belief that the new khan would not care to interfere with their liberties.

His own case was far more embarrassing: for the moment, at least. The tidings of Burah's death and his son's succession to the sovereign office of Khan had struck him like a blow. It was only the evening of the sixth day, he reflected, and Agahr had not expected anything important to happen until the seventh day, at least. How in the world had Ahmed managed to reach Mekran from Takkatu so soon?

Then the truth flashed upon him, and he groaned aloud. The tall Baluch he had rescued from the men of Raab and escorted safely to the plains of Melin was none other than Prince Ahmed himself, and Kasam's folly in interfering with his uncle Agahr's plans had resulted in his own undoing!

They were at the palace now.

Dirrag held Kasam's horse while he dismounted and then escorted the young man into the courtyard and through several winding passages. Soon they came to a small chamber, the entrance to which was guarded by the Arab slave Memendama, who allowed them to pass at a word from Dirrag. Here were more attendants and slaves, richly dressed in the crimson, white and purple of the House of Ugg. Kasam looked uneasily upon the expressionless faces, and cast himself upon a divan to await the summons to the Khan's presence. It came in a few brief moments, and Dirrag led the Prince through still another passage to a marble balcony, where two men were seated at a small table and a third stood at the carved rail looking into the gardens below.

Kasam glanced at the two who were seated and failed to recognize them. One was Merad, the Persian physician; the other the sirdar of the tribe of Ugg.

The man at the rail turned about, and Kasam knew him at once. He had been Dirrag's companion in the desert.

"I am glad to welcome you, Prince Kasam," said the khan, courteously. "Pray be seated."

He motioned toward a chair, but Kasam stood erect.

"Tell me first," said he, "whether I am to consider myself a guest or a prisoner."

"Surely not a prisoner, my cousin. I may use that title, may I not, since we are related?"

"The relation is distant," said the other, proudly. "I am of the Tribe of Raab, and for seven generations my ancestors ruled all Baluchistan."

"So I understand," returned the Khan, dryly. "They were also my ancestors, for the same royal blood flowed in the veins of Keedar Khan. But why should we speak of the past? Today, by the grace of Allah, I am myself ruler of Baluchistan."

"By treachery and cunning, rather than Allah's grace," retorted the Prince, defiantly. "Should right and justice prevail I would myself be sitting upon the throne of my forefathers."

"It is a matter of common knowledge," answered Ahmed, quietly facing the other and looking calmly down from his superior height into the passionate face of the younger man, "that neither right nor justice entitled your forefathers to rule this land. It may comfort you, cousin, to look into the history of the Tribes, concerning which you seem to be somewhat misinformed. But it is not worth arguing at present. What interests us more keenly is the condition that confronts us. Through the sad ending of Burah Khan, whose body now lies in state in the Mosque of the Angels, I am suddenly called to the throne. Because of my inexperience in affairs of state I shall need, as councillors and advisors, the assistance of all those to whom the welfare of Baluchistan is dear. Doubtless you love your country, Prince Kasam, and your European education will have given you broad and intelligent ideas of modern government. Therefore I value your friendship. Will you become my vizier, and assist me to rule my people to their greatest good?"

Kasam was astounded. The proposition, coming from one whom he had reason to consider his greatest foe, was as unexpected as it was impossible. Moreover, it indicated a weakness of character and lack of sound judgment in the new ruler that both pleased and encouraged him. Ahmed was a big and burly fellow, it was true, but he seemed as gentle as a woman. Evidently a monastery training did not stimulate virility of mind.

Kasam thought rapidly during the few moments that he stood with downcast eyes before Ahmed Khan, and his conclusions determined him upon his course of action. Then, remembering they were not alone, he glanced toward the table and encountered the physician's mocking gaze. If Ahmed was weak, here at least was a strong man. Indignant and alarmed at what he read in the dark eyes he turned to Abdul, the Sirdar of Ugg, for reassurance. That white-haired dignitary sat with composed and placid countenance quietly regarding the khan, whose words and actions alone seemed to afford him interest.

"What if I refuse?" asked Kasam, sharply, turning again to Ahmed.

"Then you will grieve me."

The Prince smiled contemptuously.

"But you will put me in prison, or assassinate me?"

"Why should I?"

"Because, if you cannot induce me to serve you, it will be wise to get me out of your way."

"I cannot believe that," returned Ahmed, gently. "The conspiracy of your uncle, Agahr, to place you upon my throne is well known to me, yet I have not even reproached him for his apparent disloyalty. I can understand that the heir of former khans would strive to regain his lost heritage, and your ambition seems to me a natural one. But I am here, and shall remain. Your adherents are weak and impotent. You could not be khan unless they were stronger than my own. Because I appreciate your disappointment I offer you the highest office within my gift. Be my vizier; trust me as I trust you, and let us be friends."

"I refuse!"

"Then you may go free, to act as you deem best."

"Free! I may go free?"

"Assuredly. I owe you that courtesy, even did I fear you, for having assisted me in the desert. My act may not balance accounts, but it will be an earnest of my gratitude."

"Let us cry quits," said Kasam, eagerly, "and start a new score. For I warn you, Ahmed Khan, that from this day I will oppose you with all my might."

Ahmed bowed. His face showed neither disappointment nor surprise, and as if he considered the interview at an end he turned again toward the railing, looking down into the flower beds and shrubbery.

Kasam hesitated, glancing at the other silent witness of the scene. The Persian was industriously rolling a cigarette. Dirrag stood with legs astride, evidently admiring his boots. But the sirdar, Abdul, seemed annoyed, and said to the Khan:

"The man openly threatens your Highness. We are not sure of his tribesmen of Raab. Would it not be well to take some action in this matter?"

"Let him go," replied the Khan, without turning.

Kasam flushed at the tone of indifference. It seemed to him that he was being treated like a child.

"The sirdar is old and wise," he exclaimed, angrily, "and the Khan of Mekran is young and foolish. Elai! the die is cast. I will go."

With this he strode from the room, and none hindered. The slaves and attendants in the outer chamber made no interference with his retreat. Although he had a vague fear that the Khan's words were insincere he traversed the halls, passed through the courtyard, and so left the palace.

A solitary attendant was leading his horse back and forth, as if awaiting him. Kasam was amused. The Khan needed a few lessons from his warlike sirdars if he wished to remain secure in his throne. The Prince mounted his horse and, filled with exultant thoughts, galloped away to the house of Agahr the Vizier.

Night had fallen by this time, and as Kasam approached he found Agahr's house dark and silent. The lamp that usually swung in the archway was unlighted; there were no slaves at the door. Kasam was seized with sudden misgivings. What if, in spite of Ahmed's assurances, the plotting vizier had fallen under the new khan's displeasure? Much depended upon Agahr, for all of Kasam's interests were in his keeping. Scarce a day had passed since Ahmed Khan had come into power; but much may happen in a day; indeed, much had happened, as he was soon to discover.

Answering his imperative summons a slave cautiously unbolted the door and, after a stealthy inspection of the visitor, admitted him with alacrity.

"Is my uncle here?" demanded Kasam.

The slave nodded, caught up a torch and turned to lead the way down a passage.

The Prince followed.

Suddenly a drapery was pushed aside and he entered a room brilliantly lighted. Agahr sat upon a divan, and beside him, her fair face scarcely concealed by her veil, was Maie. Facing them in a close drawn circle were Zarig, the Sirdar of Raab, a lean priest in a coarse woollen robe, and several men with restless faces that proved to be strangers to Kasam.

All were silent, even when the Prince, finding all eyes turned upon him, slapped his chest rather theatrically and exclaimed: "I am here!"

Maie twisted the rings upon her slender fingers; the vizier nodded gravely to his nephew and stroked his gray beard; the sirdar sprang to his feet and strode back and forth in the narrow confines of the room, pausing anon to cast a shrewd glance into Kasam's puzzled face. The others merely exchanged nods of understanding, save the priest, who frowned and fixed his eyes upon the floor.

At length the vizier broke the embarrassing silence.

"This," said he, waving a listless hand toward the new arrival, "is Kasam of Raab."

"Welcome!" said the sirdar, laconically, and resumed his stride. Without rising the others turned to bow gravely, but seemed to display little real interest.

Although at first both hurt and annoyed by the nonchalance of those assembled, the young prince was quick to decide that the conspirators were doubtless overwhelmed by the sudden death of Burah and the accession of his son Ahmed. It should be his part to instil new courage into their timid hearts.

"I have just come from an interview with the young khan," he said, seating himself in the sirdar's vacant chair and looking around the circle to note the effect of his announcement.

The company did not seem especially impressed. Perhaps, he reflected, they were aware that Dirrag had taken him to the palace directly on his arrival.

"Ahmed Khan," continued Kasam, "has offered to make me his vizier."

Ah, they were eager enough now. Every eye was turned curiously upon the young man.

"I refused," said Kasam, proudly. "I defied him to his very face, and bade him beware my power."

Agahr drew a sigh of relief, and Maie smiled. The sirdar, who had paused again, renewed his pacing.

"Friends," cried Kasam, "the die is cast. From this day I will fight Ahmed Khan for the throne of Mekran. Never will I rest until the usurper is conquered and I am master of all Baluchistan."

"A noble ambition," said the sirdar, nodding approval.

"You have my best wishes, cousin," added Maie, sweetly.

"But forbear, I pray you, my good Kasam, from telling me of your future plans," spoke Agahr, adjusting his robe carefully. "His Highness the Khan has also accorded me an interview, and offered to retain me as his vizier in case you refused the office. Therefore—"

"And you accepted?" asked the young man, indignantly.

Agahr frowned.

"I have filled the office for forty-six years," said he; "and surely none is better fitted than I for the place. Moreover, his Highness hath promised to increase my honors and reduce my labors, and since I grow old in serving the nation this consideration pleases me and renders me content."

"Yet you would serve a trickster—a weak, priest-ridden impostor—instead of me, your kinsman and a Prince of Raab?"

"The man you call weak," said Agahr, composedly, "has proven himself strong. In ruling Baluchistan from the throne of Mekran he will be masterful, energetic and supreme. Within his veins flows the blood of two mighty khans whom all the nation feared—as they will come to fear him. Had we considered Ahmed to be really weak, my Kasam, your cause would have prospered and gained adherents; but to oppose the new khan would be as foolish as it would prove vain. Already he has seized every thread of power in an iron grasp."

The company doubtless approved this speech, for all except the sirdar nodded wisely and sighed. But Zarig stopped abruptly and gave the Prince a keen look.

"You are trapped," said he, harshly; "trapped by friends and foes alike. What will you do, Prince Kasam?"

"Fight!" answered the young man, stoutly. "Even if I stand alone I will defy the son of Burah Khan. But I will not stand alone. England, the greatest of all nations, will support my cause, and Afghanistan will lend an army to fight for my standard. Before I have done with Ahmed Khan I will pull down the walls of Mekran about his ears."

Maie smiled again, and the lean priest laughed outright. But Zarig strode forward and grasped Kasam's hand.

"Words—all words!" he cried. "Yet the spirit is the spirit of conquerors, and you may count the tribe of Raab upon your side. Too long have I and my people bowed down to the men of Ugg. We are but one tribe of nine, but we have more wealth than all the others combined, and enough courage to match any force the young khan may send against us. Come, Kasam of Raab; let us leave these cowardly croakers to sun themselves in the favor of the usurper. It is our part to sound the battle-cry!"

Having delivered this bombastic speech the sirdar left the room, followed closely by Kasam, and in the stillness that followed their departure Maie, still smiling, bent forward and whispered:

"Words—all words!"

BOOK II
THE WOMAN

XI

Capture of David the Jew

"Now, girls, I want you to tell me what we're going to do," said Aunt Lucy, looking over her spectacles at Janet and Bessie, while her needle continued to ply in a jerky fashion. "Your father, Janet Moore, says he is waiting here in Mekran to get an audience with the high jumboree of this forsaken country about that nonsensical railroad; and *your* father, Bessie Warner, says we are staying here because we can't get away. Now, I want to know what it all means."

They were sitting in the cool and spacious upper chamber of a square white house which had been mysteriously placed at the disposal of the Americans the evening of their arrival in Mekran. It was comfortably furnished, with no less than a dozen native servants to wait upon them, their meals being bountiful and prepared with exact regularity. But no one about them had any knowledge of the English language, nor did any person in authority appear whom they might question by signs or otherwise. It almost seemed as if they had been established in this place by some fairy godmother who had then gone away and forgotten all about them. Their personal baggage had arrived with them, but there were no stables connected with the mansion and their entire caravan had disappeared.

"I think," said Janet, answering their chaperon, "that we are all as much puzzled as you are, Aunt Lucy."

"Puzzled!" exclaimed the old lady, indignantly; "why should we be puzzled? Aren't we free American citizens, and haven't we enough money to pay our way back to New York if we want to go?"

"It isn't that, dear," said Bessie, soothingly. "We have both the financial means and the inclination to leave Mekran. But Kasam seems to have wholly deserted us, and we don't know what has become of our horses and dromedaries and tents and other things. Even the Afghans who were employed to guard us have disappeared."

"I always had my suspicions of that Kasam," declared the old lady with a toss of her head; "and he turned out exactly as I thought he would. He's stolen the whole caravan, under our very noses, and he'd have stolen you, too, Janet Moore, if I hadn't kept an eye on him. Stolen you and put you into some harem or other, and dressed you in pink silk bloomers and a yellow crepe veil, like those creatures we saw passing the house the other day in stretchers."

Janet smiled, and Bessie burst into merry laughter.

"Oh, Auntie! those were not stretchers," she protested. "They were palanquins. And didn't the girls look lovely, nestled among their cushions!"

"Don't mention the hussies, Bessie. It's an outrage to parade such frightful depravity in the public streets."

"You know, dear," said Janet, softly, "that it is the custom in these Eastern countries to veil all females from the eyes of men, which are thought to defile the purity of young girls and married women alike. It seems to me a pretty thought, however misapplied, according reverence and sacredness to our sex that is in strong contrast to the bold freedom of more civilized communities."

"But the harems are dens of iniquity," declared Aunt Lucy, sternly.

"The harems are simply the quarters set aside for the women of the native households," replied Janet, "and they contain the mothers and daughters of families as well as the wives. Of course only the wealthier natives can afford harems, which are naturally more or less luxurious. But even the lower classes require their women to be veiled when in public."

"Swathed, you mean," snapped the elder lady. "Bandaged up to the eyes like mummies. You needn't talk to me about harems, Janet Moore; I know very well they're not respectable, and so do you. Did you ever hear of a harem in America? We wouldn't allow such things a minute! And do you mean to say these miserable Baluchi are not all Mormons?"

"They're Mahomedans, Auntie—or Sunnites, which is very much the same thing," remarked Bessie, "but if you mean that they have a plurality of wives, it's a thing that can't be proved, for Kasam says that even the law is powerless to invade the sanctity of the harem."

"Sanctity!" with a scornful snort. "And don't quote that young man—that caravan stealer—to me. What has all this to do with our imprisonment, I'd like to know? And what's going to be the end of it all? I've had enough of this place."

"We've all had enough of it," said a gloomy voice, and Allison entered and threw himself into a chair.

"Is there anything new, Allison?" asked Janet, looking at her brother anxiously.

"Not that I know of," he replied. "I've been roaming through the streets trying to find someone that can speak English; but they're all dummies in Mekran, so far as we're concerned. One fellow I met had a fine black horse—the most glorious Arabian I have seen—and he led it with a rag twisted around its neck. I offered him a whole pocketful of twenty-dollar gold pieces, but, by Jove! he just glanced at the money and shook his head. The American eagle doesn't seem to be of much account in this neck-of-the-woods."

"Where is papa?" asked Janet.

"Engaged in writing an official communication to the Khan, I suppose, on the engraved letter-head of the Commission. I believe he has left seven of these already at the royal palace."

"Don't they pay any attention to them?" asked Bessie.

"Why should they? No one in this enlightened town can speak or read English, now that Kasam has gone."

"Where do you suppose Kasam has gone to?"

"Can't say, I'm sure. Run away with our animals, I guess. I always had a suspicion your lovely prince was no better than a horse-thief."

"Nonsense!" said Bessie, indignantly. "I'm sure Kasam is not responsible for our present difficulties. It's that horrid Ahmed Khan, who got the start of Kasam while he was escorting us, and robbed him of his kingdom."

Allison's laugh sounded rather disagreeable.

"I can't understand," said he, "how any decent American girl can go into raptures over a brown-skinned Oriental, with treacherous eyes and a beastly temper. Kasam's no better than the rest of his tribe, and as for being khan, I don't believe he ever had a ghost of a show. The last we saw of him he was being escorted by the khan's guard to the palace—like a common criminal. Probably he's been in prison for the last three weeks."

"If that's the case how could he steal our caravan?" demanded Bessie, triumphantly.

"Don't ask so many questions, Bess. We're an ignorant lot of duffers, I'll admit, but the fact remains that Kasam is either a jail-bird or a horse-thief. You can take your choice."

"Do you know whose house this is, and who is entertaining us in this sumptuous way?" asked Janet, curiously.

"Haven't the faintest idea. This is certainly the land of mystery. We don't owe it to Kasam, you may be sure, for he had no idea when we entered the town where he was going to lodge us. And it can't be the mighty Khan, for he won't see us or have anything to do with the Commission or its members. Possibly it's that uncle whom Kasam used to talk about, the vizier, or something of that sort. If we could only find anyone to talk with we might discover the clue to the puzzle."

"In the meantime we're no better than prisoners," said Aunt Lucy, snappishly. "There's nothing to see if we go out and nothing to do if we stay in, and we're cut off from all the news of the world. We don't even know who's been elected President of the United States, and we can't ask a single question because nobody understands us. If you men had any gumption at all you'd hustle around and find out why we are treated in this impertinent manner. One thing's certain; unless something is done mighty soon I, for one, mean to quit the Commission and go back home—even if I have to walk and pay my own expenses!"

As the good lady paused in her speech a distant noise of drums and bells was heard, accompanied by the low rumble of a multitude of voices. The sounds gradually grew nearer, and Allison stepped out upon a balcony to see what caused it. Janet and Bessie followed him, but Aunt Lucy had aroused herself to such a pitch of indignation that she remained seated in her chair, busily endeavoring to mend the rents in her travelling skirt, caused during the stress of the long journey to Mekran, and refused to even look at "the heathens."

A procession turned the corner of the street and approached at a slow pace, while the inhabitants of the neighboring houses flocked out upon the balconies and roofs to watch it pass. First came a dozen Baluch warriors, the royal colors proclaiming them members of the tribe of Ugg. They were superbly mounted and seemed to be picked men. Following them were three dromedaries, gaily caparisoned. Two were ridden by native officers, but on the third was seated a man dressed simply in a black flowing robe confined at the waist with a silver girdle. He wore upon his head a round black cap, being shielded from the sun by a square of green silk, supported by four slender rods attached to his dromedary's saddle.

"It is the Persian! It is the great physician!" murmured the people, as this rare personage gazed about him and with dignified bows returned the greetings.

All in Mekran had heard the wondrous story of this mystic who had caused Burah Khan to live six days longer than the fates had decreed, and all united in honoring him.

Surging on either side of the dromedaries came a rabble beating upon gongs and jingling bells while they shouted extravagant compliments to Merad the Persian.

The remainder of the procession consisted of fifty tribesmen, fully armed and wearing the colors of the khan. Several heavily laden camels at the end implied that the caravan was setting upon a long journey.

As the Persian came opposite the house of the Americans the physician turned his dark eyes for a moment upon the balcony, and they met those of Allison.

"Good God!" cried the young man, starting back as if in terror. At the same time Janet gave a low moan and sank fainting into Bessie's arms.

"What is it? What has happened?" asked the girl, in frightened tones. "Aunt Lucy, come and help me! Janet has fainted."

While they carried her into the room and fussed over her, as women will on such occasions, Allison turned and rushed down into the street. He was not long in overtaking the dromedaries, and, running beside them, he shouted:

"Wait, doctor! Let me speak to you a moment!"

The Persian was bowing in the direction of a balcony on the opposite side of the street, and seemed not to hear the young American. But Allison was desperate.

"Wait—wait!" he cried again, and turned to seize the camel's bridle.

Then the physician slowly turned his head and gazed curiously down upon the man.

"I must speak with you," said Allison, tugging at the bridle.

The Persian seemed puzzled but smiled indulgently and glanced toward his attendants. Instantly a big Baluch rode forward and grasped Allison by his collar, thrusting him back into the crowd.

The procession moved on, the honored Persian again bowing to right and left and wholly indifferent to the cries the American sent after him. When the last pack animal had passed, Allison's guard released him; but the engineer followed with dogged steps until the caravan had reached the iron gateway and passed through without halting, the noisy rabble shouting enthusiastic farewells as it disappeared. Then silent and thoughtful, Allison returned to the house.

"Without doubt I have been mistaken," he mused; "and yet it seems strange that the world should contain two men whose features are identically the same—and both of them physicians, too. In New York

Osborne passed for an East Indian, and this man is a Persian. If they were the same surely he would have recognized me, if only to curse me as he did at home in the old days."

He found Janet not only recovered but laughing gaily at what she called her "foolish weakness." Somehow it jarred upon Allison to hear his melancholy sister laughing, to note the sparkle in her eyes and the flush that for the first time in years mantled her fair cheeks. He had no difficulty in accounting for all this, yet when she cast an eager, enquiring look at her brother he took a certain satisfaction in answering it with a scowl and a shake of his head.

"I followed him," said he, "and managed to speak to him. We were both mistaken, Janet. It is a stranger—some notable the people seem to know well, and call by the name of Merad."

"Merad?"

"Yes. He has started upon a journey across the plains—returning to his home, I think."

To his surprise Janet smiled and began twisting up her disordered hair.

"Very well, dear," she answered, carelessly, and as if dismissing the subject from her mind as unimportant she turned to renew her conversation with Bessie.

Suddenly a scuffle was heard in the passage.

"I've got him! I've got him!" called the voice of Dr. Warner; and then the draperies were pulled aside and the Colonel and the doctor rushed into the room dragging between them a nondescript form from which came yells of protest in a high minor key.

"We've got him!" shouted the Colonel, triumphantly, as the prisoner was dumped in the center of the room.

"Land of mercy! What *have* you got?" demanded Aunt Lucy, glaring upon the strange object with amazement.

The doctor drew out his handkerchief and mopped his forehead vigorously.

"He speaks English!" he answered, impressively, waving the handkerchief in the direction of the limp captive.

Janet laughed, almost hysterically; but the others stared with marked interest at the man who could speak English.

He was exceedingly short in stature, and likewise exceedingly squat and round of form. His head was entirely bald except for a bushy lock upon the very top, but a long beard, tangled, unkempt and grizzled, reached nearly to his middle. His cheeks were fat, his eyes small and beady, and his nose so curved that its point was perpetually lost in the flowing beard. For costume the man wore a gown of red and white quilted silk that Aunt Lucy afterward declared reminded her of a bath robe, except that no word signifying "bath" could ever be properly applied to either the robe or the wearer. There were sandals upon his grimy feet and a leathern pouch hung at his girdle.

"Wherever in the world did you get him?" asked Bessie, drawing a long breath.

"Energy and enterprise will accomplish anything," replied the doctor, proudly. "The Colonel and I went to the booths this morning to search for tobacco. All the shops in this infernal town are mere booths, you know, and all are located against the inner side of the city wall. Until today we had never visited any of these places except the nearest ones, for they all look alike. But good tobacco is a scarce article in Mekran, and we kept circling around the wall until we came to one dirty little hole where this man sat. To our surprise and joy he answered us in English. We fell on his neck—I believe the Colonel kissed him—and then we seized him and brought him here."

"I do not remember kissing him," retorted the Colonel, with twinkling eyes. "It must have been the doctor."

"Oh, Luther!" said Aunt Lucy, horrified. "How could you ever do it?"

"He speaks English," replied the doctor. "We've adopted him."

A whine came from the prostrate victim.

"What's his name?" asked Allison.

"Hi, there. What's your name?" questioned the doctor, stirring the bundle with his foot.

"Davit, goot Excellency," came the meek reply.

"Stand up, David, so we can get a good look at you," said the Colonel.

So David rolled over and with some difficulty scrambled to his feet. Miss Warner began to giggle, and Janet laughed outright. Even Aunt Lucy allowed a grim smile to rest upon her wrinkled features.

"Who are you, David?" enquired the doctor.

"I iss merchant, most Excellency. Chew merchant."

"Where did you learn English?"

"From mine fadder, who vas a Cherman merchant unt lived in Kelat."

"Who taught him English?"

David looked reproachful.

"He knew it, most High Excellency. Mine fadder could shbeak anyt'ing efferyvhere."

"Except the truth, I suppose. Tell me, David; are you rich?"

The Jew cast a frightened look around him.

"All I haf in de vorlt," he moaned, "iss in my pouch. If you rob de pouch I am nodding anymore whateffer!"

The Colonel with a sudden motion grasped the pouch and jerked it free from the girdle. Then, while David wept real tears of anguish, his tormentor emptied the contents of the pouch upon the table. These consisted of a miscellaneous collection of native coins of very little value.

"Really, you are very poor, David," the Colonel remarked.

"I am vorse, goot Excellency," he replied, encouraged by the tone. "Who iss so misserable ass Davit? Who iss so poor, so frientless, so efferyt'ing? I shall go dead!"

"Don't do that, David. If a man is poor, he should strive to get rich. Watch me," and the Colonel took a handful of gold from his pocket and threw it into the pouch, afterward adding the former insignificant contents. The injunction to watch this proceeding was wholly unnecessary. David's eyes sparkled like diamonds and he trembled with eagerness while the Colonel carefully tied the mouth of the pouch. Then, tossing the bag from hand to hand so that it jingled merrily, he said:

"This is real wealth, David—good yellow gold. And it shall all be yours, with an equal sum added to it, if you consent to serve us faithfully."

David fell upon his knees and waved his short arms frantically toward the pouch.

"I vill do anyt'ing, great Excellency! I vill be serfant—I vill be slafe! Yes, I vill be brudder to you all!"

"Very good," returned the Colonel. He walked to a massive cabinet, elaborately carved, that was built into the wall of the room. Unlocking a drawer he tossed the pouch within and then carefully relocked it and placed the key in his own pocket.

There was a look of despair on David's face. He still knelt upon the floor, his arms rigidly outstretched toward the cabinet.

"Now, David," continued the Colonel, calmly, while the others looked on, much amused, "you must not forget that you are going to be very rich, and that all this money—doubled, and perhaps tripled—will be yours as soon as you have earned it. And you are going to earn it by speaking English, and translating our speech to natives, and by doing exactly what we tell you to do, at all times and under all circumstances.

But if you deceive me—if you prove unfaithful in anyway—you will never see your pouch again."

"I vill shpik Engliss all day! I vill do anyt'ing!" protested David.

"Once," said the doctor, "a man proved faithless to us. And what do you suppose happened to him, David? Well, you couldn't guess. I skinned him very carefully and stuffed him with sawdust, and now he sits on a shelf in my home with a lovely smile on his face and two glass eyes that all observers consider very beautiful."

David groaned.

"I am true man, most Excellency! I half neffer deceive. I neffer *can* deceive!

"We shall trust you," said the doctor, gravely. "I feel quite certain you will never deserve to be stuffed with sawdust."

"How absurd!" exclaimed Aunt Lucy. "Do give him a bath and some decent clothes, and stop bothering him. If we've got to have the fellow around let's make him respectable."

"That is a task that can only be performed outwardly," returned the doctor, imperturbably. "But even that is worthy of consideration. Come, Allison, let us see what can be done toward the renovation of David."

As the shuffling form of "the man who could speak English" disappeared through the archway, Aunt Lucy, who had been shrewdly studying his face, remarked oracularly:

"He's playing possum. You mark my words, that Jew's no fool. If he was, he wouldn't be a Jew."

XII

The Girl on the Divan

N ow this," said the Colonel, "is to be a council of war. We are in grave difficulties, and may as well look the matter straight in the face."

The little band of Americans seemed all to agree with him, for it was with fitting gravity that they turned their eyes upon the leader of the Commission—all except Aunt Lucy, whose wondering gaze was full upon little David, resplendent in his new costume. David's outer robe was orange and white, and his inner garb brilliant green. An orange turban was twisted around his bald head and orange hose covered his stubby legs. This gorgeousness was due to a whim of the doctor, and it appeared to be eminently satisfactory to David. A native barber had trimmed and curled his straggling beard and the Jew had been scrubbed and scented so thoroughly that he had a fresh and wholesome look which was in strong contrast to his former unkempt condition.

"If he is to be our emissary and interpreter," the doctor had said, "he must be made worthy of the great Commission, and in this barbarous country color is everything."

"Then," replied Aunt Lucy, "David is everything. He reminds me of a brass band on parade."

David was now present at the council, seated between the Colonel and the doctor.

"In the first place," resumed the leader, "we must acknowledge that we are virtually prisoners in this town, possessing no means in the way of animals or attendants of getting away. David has talked with the servants in this house and has discovered that we are guests of his Highness the Khan, who has ordered us supplied with every comfort that can be procured. Why the khan has taken an interest in our affairs—we being entire strangers to him—is a deep mystery. Unless he feels that he owes us some compensation for having driven Kasam out of Mekran."

"Did he drive Kasam out?" asked Bessie.

"I understand from David that there is room for but one on the throne, and Ahmed Khan naturally prefers to sit there himself. So our friend Kasam made tracks and left us to shift for ourselves. All of the tribe of Raab, a powerful clan in Baluchistan, have deserted Ahmed and joined Kasam, who is in open revolt."

"Would it not be safer for us to leave here and join Prince Kasam?" enquired Bessie.

"Why, I'm inclined to think, from the gossip David has picked up, that Kasam's cause is a forlorn one, and that he's not particularly safe himself. Ahmed Khan may wake up some day and poke him with a sharp stick. Moreover, there's no disguising the fact that when our guide left Mekran and set up in business for himself he deliberately robbed us of the beasts we had bought and paid for with our own money, besides carrying off our Afghans, whose pay was fortunately in arrears. The Prince couldn't well have treated us with less consideration, and in strong contrast with his actions Ahmed Khan has come to the front like a man and taken care of us. Let's pin our faith to Ahmed Khan."

"Cannot we induce Ahmed to supply us with a caravan?" asked Allison.

"That's the point. That is, it's one point. We mustn't lose sight of the fact that we came here to get a right of way for the railroad. The first concession to get from the Khan is the right of way. The means to journey back to the railway at Quettah is the second consideration, although no less important. These things being accomplished, we will have performed our duty to the Syndicate and to ourselves."

"When will they be accomplished?" enquired Aunt Lucy, in brisk, matter-of-fact tones.

"Ahem! That I cannot say, to a day, my dear Mrs. Higgins. The fact is, I've sent David twice to the Khan, with demands in writing for an interview. But David can't get within a mile of the Khan, notwithstanding his impressive costume—which cost eight fillibees, native money."

"The Khan," added the doctor musingly, "is quite an exclusive personage. His Highness' guards have threatened to tattoo our dear David unless he ceases to bother them."

David groaned, thereby concurring in this statement.

"Then what is to be done?" asked Janet, who had displayed a lively interest in her father's discourse.

The Colonel shook his head, rather despondently.

"What do you suggest, David?" asked the doctor.

David had been earnestly regarding the cabinet in which his gold was stored. Now, however, being addressed, he reluctantly withdrew his eyes from the vicinity of his treasure, heaved a deep sigh as if awakening from a happy dream, and said:

"Vy nod try de vizier?"

"What vizier?"

"De grant vizier, Agahr. He iss de biggest man here ven der Khan he iss somevhere else."

"That seems a practical hint," said the Colonel. "I'll write a new letter, addressed to the vizier."

David turned uneasily in his seat.

"Letters, most Excellency, iss a bad vay. Noboddy takes letters to Agahr de vizier. Dey go talk mit Agahr."

"Will he see people?"

"Vy nod? He iss vizier."

"Then one of us had best go and interview him, and take David along for interpreter," decided the Colonel promptly.

"He speaks such lovely English!" added Aunt Lucy, with a toss of her head.

"The vizier won't hear his English," said the doctor, "and I suspect David's native dialect is somewhat clearer and more comprehensive. Otherwise he'd have been murdered long ago. Now then, who'll tackle the vizier?"

"I'll go," replied Allison, to the surprise of all. "I'm tired of hanging around doing nothing, and this mission promises a bit of excitement."

"Very good," said his father, pleased at the remark. "Be firm with him, Allison. Insist upon his securing an interview for me with the Khan, and also tell the vizier we want a caravan to take us to Quettah. Let him understand we have plenty of money to pay for what we require."

"I'll do the best I can," said Allison. "Come, David."

AGAHR HAD JUST AWAKENED FROM his afternoon siesta and was sitting with Maie in a cool, darkened room. Both the vizier and his daughter were in a happy mood.

"There has been a more agreeable atmosphere at the palace since the Persian physician went away," said the old man. "The fellow had a suspicious manner of looking at me, as if he knew all my secret thoughts and intended to betray them."

"I hate the man!" exclaimed Maie, with a shiver of her rounded shoulders.

"And I," answered Agahr. "But he is gone. Let us hope he will never return."

"Yet the Khan liked him?" said the girl, enquiringly.

"They were old friends, although their ages differ so widely; and there is a secret between them, of some sort. The physician, who dominated everyone else, was very gentle with Ahmed."

"That was his cunning," declared Maie. "It is not wise to attempt to rule Ahmed Khan." She broke off suddenly, and nestling closer to Agahr upon the divan she asked, in soft accents: "Do you think he is attracted toward me, my father?"

"He has eyes for no one else when you are by," returned the vizier, fondly caressing the girl's hand. "But that is not strange, my Maie. You are more beautiful than the houris of Paradise."

She sighed, very gently, as if the tribute was sweet.

"And how does Ahmed Khan spend his days?" she enquired. "Do the dancing girls still amuse him?"

"He has sent all the dancing girls away," was the reply, "and every inmate of Burah's harem, both young and old, has been conveyed by Melka to the Castle of Ugg, far away in the South country."

"I wonder why?" said the girl, thoughtfully. "Perhaps, having been a priest so long, he does not care for women."

Agahr smiled.

"Then why is he improving and beautifying the harem? he asked.

"Is he?" she cried, starting up.

"The apartments of the women were turned over to an army of workmen a week ago. In another week the harem will be beautiful beyond compare. And the gardens and Court of the Maidens are being made magnificent with rare plants and exquisite flowers. That is not an indication, my beauty, that the Khan does not care for women."

"True," she returned, and sat as if lost in thought. Then she asked:

"What woman, besides myself, has the Khan looked kindly upon?"

"None," answered the vizier, without hesitation. "It was only this morning he spoke to me of you, asking how many summers you had seen and saying you were rarely beautiful."

She smiled contentedly.

"How wise we were, oh my father, to abandon the cause of the Pretender and ally ourselves with Ahmed Khan."

"Kasam is too weak and unreliable to become a leader of men," returned the vizier, calmly.

"Yet for years—while Burah Khan grew aged—I imagined I should become the queen of Kasam's harem, and plotted shrewdly to place him upon the throne. Is it not amusing, my father, to remember that I learned to speak the awkward English tongue, just because Kasam had lived in England and spoke that language?"

"It was time wasted," said the vizier. "But that reminds me that those American travellers are still in Mekran. I wonder why the Khan is keeping them."

Maie started.

"Are there not women among them?" she asked.

"Two or three of the party are women."

"Are they beautiful?"

Agahr laughed, and pinched her cheek.

"There are no beautiful women but ours," he returned, "and of them you are the queen, my Maie! However, jealous one, the Khan has never looked upon these foreign women, nor does he care to."

"Then why does he keep the Americans here? Will he permit them to build their railway?"

"Indeed, no," said the vizier. "He agrees with me that a railway would ruin our country. But why he will neither see the Americans nor permit them to depart from Mekran is really a mystery."

"Ah, I must discover it!" the girl exclaimed, earnestly. "When a thing is not understood it is dangerous. And it is well to beware of all women, even though they be foreigners and ugly of form and feature. I can manage any man who lives, my father, be he khan or vizier," with a smile into his face; "but even the far-seeing Prophet failed to understand my sex aright."

"I have put a spy in the household of the Americans," said Agahr.

"Whom?"

"David the Jew."

"David is clever," said Maie, thoughtfully. "But will he be faithful? Gold is his only master."

"I have promised, if David is faithful, to purchase from him those wonderful African pearls—at his own price. That will make him rich, and the pearls will be your bridal gift, my daughter."

She clasped her hands, ecstatically.

"And the great diamond that David brought from Algiers? What of that?"

"The Khan himself has purchased it, by my advice."

"Then it shall be mine!" she whispered. "You have done well, my father. How long has David been with the Americans?"

"Three days. I expect him here, presently, for the foreigners begin to grow impatient of restraint, and I have told David to let me quiet them with promises."

"Question the Jew closely when he comes, concerning the Americans. I must know more of them, and we must watch them closely."

The vizier arose, arranged his robe, and with slow steps left the room to cross a passage that admitted him to the apartment wherein he was wont to receive visitors on affairs of state. The fringe of the drapery caught as he threw it back, and hung partially open behind him; but neither he nor Maie, who still reclined upon her divan, noted this.

Scarcely was Agahr seated in his great velvet-lined chair of state when a slave entered to announce the arrival of David and the young American, who desired an audience.

The vizier hesitated, in deep thought, mindful of Maie's injunctions. Finally he said to the slave:

"Admit David the Jew to my presence; but tell him the American must wait in the outer chamber until he is summoned."

So presently little David entered the room, drawing the draperies closely behind him and then turning to bow cringingly before the vizier.

Allison waited impatiently. Why should Agahr wish to speak with David in secret? It looked decidedly suspicious, thought the young man, and after a few moments he arose and glanced down the passage. He seemed to be entirely alone, and the heavy rugs would deaden any sound of footsteps.

Stealthily he made his way down the passage toward the crimson draperies that had fallen behind David's pudgy form. On his way he passed an entrance on the opposite side, to which the curtain hung half open, displaying the dim interior of the room. And then he paused as if fascinated, his eyes fixed upon the most exquisite picture he had ever beheld.

Maie lay carelessly stretched upon the divan, her robe thrown back, her arms crossed behind her head and the outlines of her rounded limbs showing daintily through the folds of soft mulle that enveloped them. Her eyes, languid and dark, gazed full into those of the intruder, and as she noted his enraptured face she smiled in a way that instantly robbed Allison of all caution or even a realization of his delicate position in this household. In two strides he was by her side, kneeling at the divan and clasping the unresisting hands of the girl in both his own.

"Oh, my darling!" he whispered, looking deep into the lustrous eyes, "how very, very beautiful you are!"

Such sincere tribute was beyond Maie's power to resist. The little head might be full of ambitions, schemes and intrigues, yet there was room for a vivid appreciation of man's adoration, and this abrupt method of wooing was sure to appeal to her Eastern imagination. She sighed, forgetful of all save the handsome face bent over her, and only the sound of her father's stern voice coming from the opposite chamber had power to recall her to the present.

"You must go, my American," she said, in clear English, "or you will be discovered."

"Ah, you speak my language?" said Allison, in delight; "then you will understand me, sweet one, when I tell you how lovely you are—how passionately I adore you!"

He clasped his arms around her and drew her so close that her bosom rested against his own. The red lips were nearer now—so near that he kissed them again and again, in a very abandon of ecstatic joy.

"They will find you," said Maie, softly. "And they will kill you."

"What does it matter?" he rejoined, recklessly. "One moment such as this is worth a hundred deaths!"

With a sudden movement she freed herself from his embrace and sat up, facing him.

"Take this key," she whispered, drawing it from her bosom, where it was secured by a silken thread. "It unlocks the Gate of the Griffins, at the end of our garden. Meet me there tonight—an hour before midnight—and take care you are seen by no prying eye. And now, go—and go quickly!"

She broke the thread and handed him a tiny silver key, which he thrust into his pocket.

"One kiss, sweetheart," he begged; "just one more to comfort me until—"

"Go, or all is lost," she answered, almost fiercely, and seizing his arm she dragged him to another doorway and thrust him from the room with a force her slender form did not seem to warrant.

It was time. Allison heard footsteps and voices, and staggering through an ante-room he barely had time to reach the outer chamber and throw himself into a chair when David and a slave entered.

"Hiss goot Excellency, de vizier, vill see you," said David, looking with open surprise into Allison's flushed and excited face.

"I must have fallen asleep, David," said the American, reaching out his arms as if to stretch them, "for I dreamed I was in Paradise, and you were imploring the Prophet to pardon my sins."

David grinned, and turned to lead him to the vizier. But the Jew's keen eyes had made a hasty survey of the room, and noted a curtain swaying gently where no breeze could ever have reached it.

XIII

A Wild Wooing

W ell?" asked the Colonel; "what luck?"

"None at all," growled Allison. "The vizier is as tricky and sly as his master. He assumed a dignified and benevolent air, was very sorry we were discontented, but can do nothing to help us."

"How about horses?"

"The vizier states it is an ecclesiastical command that no beasts of burden shall be sold to an infidel, under pain of death. His Highness the Khan regrets it; His Excellency the Vizier regrets it. You are referred to Aboullah O'Brien, Grand Mufti of the Mosque of the Angels, who issued the order to the faithful."

"It iss Aboullah Beyren," corrected David, meekly.

"How long has this order been in effect?" enquired the doctor.

"Since the day we arrived. It was not aimed at us, by any means. It was a coincidence."

"That looks bad," said the Colonel gravely. "How about my interview with the Khan?"

"The vizier will intercede for you. He will go down on his knees to His Supreme Mightiness; he will implore the Star of the Heavens to see you. But he doubts if we ever get within earshot of the Glorious and Magnificent Defender of the Faith, who is otherwise known as Ahmed Khan. It seems he has other fish to fry, and is busy getting them ready. We can do nothing with the scoundrelly vizier, I am certain."

"Then we must depend upon David to get me an audience with the Khan. Americans are not accustomed to fail in what they undertake. See here, David," turning to that worthy merchant; "can't you bribe your way into the royal palace?"

"I will try, most Excellency," answered David, eagerly. "But de bribe must be great moneys—grant moneys—many golt fillibees! Unt I promise nodding. Maybe I see de Khan; maybe nod. Who can tell?"

"It sounds like a risky investment, David," remarked the doctor. "We'll take time to think it over."

They thought of many things, in the days that followed, but could arrive at no plan that promised to provide a caravan or give them an opportunity to negotiate with the Khan concerning the new railway.

The Colonel went personally to the palace one day, taking along the trembling David as interpreter. The official who met him at the entrance listened to him respectfully, but assured him that no message from an infidel could be carried to the Khan. Hints of money had no effect. It would cost him his head to disturb the Khan on such an errand.

Under these unfortunate conditions the Colonel began to be worried, and even the doctor lost much of his habitual cheerfulness. Aunt Lucy vowed vengeance upon every barbarian in Baluchistan, and promised the United States would wipe this miserable country off the map as soon as she returned and reported their treatment to her friend the senator.

But Allison, to the wonder of all, stopped grumbling and bore his imprisonment with rare fortitude and good nature. Janet also grew brighter and merrier day by day—a circumstance that did much toward reconciling her father to their enforced stay in Mekran. Bessie, always philosophic and gay, made no complaint of any sort. And so the days passed swiftly away and as yet brought no change in the fortunes of the stranded Commission.

One evening David came in greatly excited. A messenger had arrived from the Khan. Although that haughty potentate still ignored the Commission he had placed two saddle horses from his own stables at the disposal of the young ladies. If they would ride at daybreak on the following morning—that hour being the most cool and delightful of the day—the Khan would send a competent guard to protect them. His Most Serene and Magnificent Highness offered this courtesy in order to relieve the monotony of the young ladies' stay in his capital. He made no mention of the other members of the party, who might exist as monotonously as ever. And the messenger awaited an answer.

This was, indeed, a startling proposition. Eastern women did not ride, yet the Khan seemed to know that nothing could be more acceptable to American girls than a dash across country on the back of a spirited horse. They were very glad to accept the favor, and the Colonel hoped it might lead in some way to more friendly relations between them and the ruler of Mekran, and perhaps result in the interview he so ardently desired.

"But who's going to chaperon them?" enquired Aunt Lucy. "It seems I'm not invited."

The Colonel thought the khan's guard would be sufficient.

"But it's a heathen country, and they'll have to bandage their faces," declared the old lady.

"We'll wear veils until we are out of Mekran," said Bessie. "Then there will be no masculine eyes to see us, and we'll take them off."

So at daybreak Janet and Bessie were ready for their ride, and soon a grizzled Baluch warrior rode up to the house leading two magnificent bays from the famous stables of Mehmet. The one that Janet rode was the very animal that had carried Ahmed on his swift journey from the monastery, and Bessie's horse was but little inferior.

The warrior saluted and assisted the ladies to mount. It was Dirrag. He led them through the streets, around the palace enclosure and out at the south gate. A beautiful country lay spread before them, and as the keen morning air saluted their nostrils, brightened their eyes and flushed their cheeks, the girls dashed away at a canter with Dirrag silently following a few paces behind.

After their long confinement within the walls of a city dwelling this free, invigorating exercise was a great delight to the two girls, and they enjoyed the ride thoroughly. Passing through the city on their return they closely veiled their faces, yet were evidently objects of curiosity to those of the natives who were abroad so early.

Dirrag held the stirrups for them to dismount and then silently touched his cap and led the horses back to the khan's stables. But next morning he was again at their door with the mounts, and their ride became a daily event to the girls.

Dirrag knew no English, but Janet and Bessie had come to understand many of the Baluch words—a dialect evidently founded upon Arabic—and could even speak a few simple sentences, learned by contact with the native servants and somewhat puzzling explanations from David. So the silence of their first rides began to be broken by laconic observations on the part of the battered old warrior, who seemed not to object to acting as escort to the charming infidel women. Occasionally they passed the house of Agahr the Vizier and Maie, who was informed of all that occurred in the capital, watched from her latticed window the graceful forms of the American girls riding by and on several occasions when they neglected to arrange their veils caught glimpses of their fair faces.

It was enough to set the vizier's daughter wild with envy and chagrin. Why should the Khan favor these outcasts-these women of another world? Was it for them the harem was being prepared, despite her father's protestation that Ahmed had never seen the foreign women nor ever would see them? The girl well knew that their beauty could in no way compare with her own in the eyes of any true Baluch. The Americans were deformed by being laced and belted at the waist and wearing heavy, close-fitting draperies that must not only be uncomfortable but were decidedly ugly in appearance. But Maie could not deny they sat their horses gracefully and with rare self-possession, and men have queer ideas of beauty. Perhaps Ahmed Khan might admire the novelty of their white faces, their queerly arranged hair and the pink finger nails that lacked any trace of the beautifying henna.

Maie was jealous, and with good reason. She had abandoned her handsome cousin Kasam for the more powerful and scarcely less handsome Ahmed Khan, and if fate destined her to lose them both she was surely to be pitied.

But her father declared he had no such fears. Ahmed was difficult to understand, it was true; but Ahmed was a man, and he had seen and admired Maie. Was he not beautifying his harem? and what place could these stiff Americans have amid the luxuries of the perfumed baths, the gardens of the Court of the Maidens, or the musk-scented cushions of the oriental divans? It would be as absurd as putting a frog in the jar devoted to gold-fish. Add to this argument the fact that Maie was the most beautiful maiden the world had ever known, and none but a fool could fail to read the lines of destiny.

One morning Dirrag turned to the west, and led his fair companions across the valley and up the curve of the long hill that enclosed it. The country was more wild and unsettled here than at the south or east, and when finally they mounted the brow of the hill and gazed down into the next valley Dirrag pointed out a cluster of white dots showing far away against the green of the fertile plains.

"Kasam," said he.

The girls looked with eager interest.

"Is it a camp?" asked Bessie, twisting her tongue into the Baluch dialect.

Dirrag seemed to understand.

"Kasam is a rebel," he said, looking calmly at the tents. "Many traitors to our great khan have joined him. His army grows daily. It will be battle, some day, and Kasam and his host will disappear like snow before the sun."

"Has the Khan also an army?" asked Janet.

Dirrag smiled, proudly.

"The warriors of Mekran are as numerous as the leaves in the forest. Our mighty khan does not mind Kasam, for the buzzing of a bee against the window-pane is not annoying. But when the time comes he will crush the rebel in a day."

"That may not be so easy," exclaimed Bessie, while her eyes sparkled indignantly. "Prince Kasam is no child I'll bet he knows very well what he's about!"

Dirrag shrugged his shoulders. He did not understand, for in her excitement she spoke in English. But other ears heard the words, and a young man rode out from a clump of trees that had concealed him and advanced toward the ladies with a bow and a smile.

It was Kasam himself, mounted upon a magnificent gelding that was black as night. He wore a native costume, sparkling with jewels, and looked as handsome and manly as any prince in a fairy tale.

Dirrag, frowning and alert, drew his terrible curved cimeter and prepared to defend his charges. But the girls were pleased at the encounter, and Bessie managed to cry out in Baluch: "Don't strike, Dirrag! It is Prince Kasam."

"Good reason to strike," growled the warrior; but he stood at attention, awaiting the outcome of the adventure and admiring secretly the enemy's boldness.

"I thank you, fair ladies, for your protection," said Kasam, speaking gaily and in English. "Not that I particularly fear your doughty champion, but because it affords me the opportunity I have longed for to talk frankly with you, and explain why I seemingly abandoned you on the eve of your arrival in Mekran."

"And also why you carried away our entire caravan," added Janet, severely.

Kasam laughed.

"All is fair in love and war," he rejoined. "You did not need the caravan any longer, and I needed it badly. It was natural I should take advantage of your good nature and my own necessities. Look!" pointing proudly to the plain below; "it is the encampment of my army—the host that is to win for me the throne of Mekran!"

"Are our horses and dromedaries there? And our escort of Afghans?" asked Janet.

"All are there. For the money loss you have sustained I can easily recompense you. As for my own desertion, I agreed to guide your party to Mekran, and I kept my promise. Really, I cannot see that you have just cause for complaint."

"We have no way to leave the city," replied Janet. "Your act has made us prisoners in Mekran."

"That was part of my plan," declared the young man, eyeing the girl with open admiration. "I do not want you to leave Mekran until I am khan."

"Why?" she asked.

He hesitated, and glanced at Dirrag.

"Let us ride on," he said, "and, if you will kindly pace beside me, Miss Janet, I will confide to your ears alone my hopes and ambitions."

He reached out and caught the rein of her bridle, drawing the horse beside his own, and then he rode slowly down the hill toward the city. Dirrag, puzzled by the action and marvelling that the Prince should venture so near the khan's headquarters, followed a few paces behind Kasam, with Bessie at his side. The girl's face had flushed red at Kasam's evident preference for her friend, and her lips were pressed ominously together. She nodded approval as she saw that the warrior beside her still held his drawn cimeter tightly clasped in his hand, for the stern look upon his grim features boded no good to the rebel prince.

For a few paces Kasam rode in silence; then, glancing behind to make sure they were not overheard, he said:

"Miss Moore—Janet! the conditions that surround me oblige me to be frank with you, and to discard all foolish formalities. Although I have been educated in London you must not forget I am a native Baluch, and that we of the East are children of impulse, obeying the dictates of our hearts spontaneously and scorning that cold formality so much affected by your race. I have neither the time nor the opportunity to woo you in the dignified Western fashion. But I love you; and, after all, that is enough for a man to say!"

"Prince Kasam!"

"Since you must hear me, pray rob your voice of its scorn, my love. Be sweet and fond as a woman should. Let your real soul peep out of your beautiful eyes—let your heart bound wild and free in unison with my own. We are man and woman, fitted to sweet communion one with the other and destined to be happy in the passionate union of our lives." His voice was broken and excited; his eyes sparkled with fierce intensity; the conventionality of the Western civilization he had once known was all forgotten. "I love you—I adore you, my Janet! And I am a prince—soon to be Khan of all this great land. Speak to me, dear one! Promise to leave all else and cling to me alone—to follow my fortunes until I can place you in the palace where you shall be queen!"

"You have taken me by surprise, Prince Kasam," said Janet, gravely. "I am sorry you have spoken in this way."

"And why?" he cried. "Can love be denied when it clamors at the door of an eager heart? Why should I not love you? Why should you not accept my love?"

She looked into his animated face and smiled sadly.

"Because I do not belong to myself," she answered, trying hard, as a true woman will, to soften the blow. "Can I give you what another claims as his right?"

She should have said more, or not so much; but she did not know the Baluch temper.

He drew a quick breath at her words and reined his horse to a sudden halt. Her own horse stopped at the same time, and for one long moment Kasam gazed steadily into the fair face she turned pleadingly upon him.

With an exclamation and a passionate gesture he spurred forward. The black gelding was off like the wind across the plain, and Janet was left to stare wonderingly after him.

Dirrag swore heartily; but the native oaths, lacking translation, did not offend the ears of the American girls. The warrior dared not leave his companions to pursue the prince, who circled around and made straight for the hillside in the direction of his encampment.

An embarrassing silence fell upon the three as they again rode forward. Dirrag was plainly suspicious of Janet's secret conference with the rebel, and Bessie's sweet face was masked with a grieved and despondent expression that was new to it.

But Janet was too preoccupied to notice her friend's distress, nor did she deign to explain, even with a word, her strange interview with Kasam.

XIV

THE VEILED WOMAN

What does it mean?" demanded Maie, stamping her small foot in passion. "Tell me at once, my father—what does it mean?"

The vizier sat doubled up in his chair a picture of abject humiliation and despair. His chin lay inert against his chest; the white beard streamed to his waist, where long and bony fingers clutched it and dragged at the meshes nervously; his eyes refused to meet the glowing orbs his incensed daughter turned upon him like searchlights baring the soul.

"Will you speak?" she asked, scornfully. "Will you speak, most sublime and magnificent Vizier—if only to proclaim yourself an ass?"

"Have peace—have peace!" muttered Agahr, moving uneasily. "How was I to know that Merad the Persian would return?"

"Oh trusting and childlike servant—thou one innocent in all the world of guile!"

"Ahmed tells no one of his plans," the vizier went on, heedless of her jibes; "nor can I be expected to probe the secret thoughts of the Khan. When Merad departed there was no hint of his mission or that he expected soon to return. My spy waits in Ahmed's private chamber; my spy serves his every meal; my spy listens to the secret conferences he holds with sirdars and officers of the household. If the Khan sneezes, I know it; if he stirs abroad my eyes follow his every step. But his thoughts, being known only to himself and to Allah, baffle my efforts, and the jargon he speaks to the foreign physician is a language none else can understand."

Maie clutched at her silken scarf and rent its folds in twain, twisting and tearing the tender fabric until its threads lay scattered in all directions.

"I hate him! I have hated him from the first," she said. "Aye, even as I clasped his clammy form in my arms, and knew that water rather than blood flowed in his veins, I loathed the man and guessed he would strive to ruin me!"

"You did this?" asked the vizier, sternly. "You clasped the Persian in your arms—a man so old that he might call you daughter? You played the wanton with this stranger?"

"Even so," she answered, mockingly. "I would have sacrificed anything, at that time, to have cut old Burah's thread of life. But, elai! your cold Persian would not respond. He spurned me from him. I was very safe in his presence, my father."

Agahr's brows did not unbend. He eyed his daughter with a look of smouldering fury.

"Hear me, Maie," he commanded; "you are the child of my heart, my best beloved. With you I have plotted and intrigued until my very soul is stained with evil in the Prophet's sight; but all for your future glory and pride, and with no thought of my own advantage. But if you disregard your own purity, if I find that you give yourself to strange men or humble me in the sight of Allah, I swear to kill you as quickly as I would a dog of an infidel! Aye, my own slaves shall cut you down like a noxious weed."

She laughed then, showing her dimples and her pearl-like teeth; but the laugh rang hard in Agahr's ears.

"What man has knowledge to teach a woman?" she asked, with a careless gesture. "Is your wisdom so little, my father, that you judge me lacking in worldly cunning? Bah! have comfort, then! Never can you plot so well for Maie as Maie can plot for herself. And when I fall the heavens shall follow in my wake. Enough of this. We face a real trouble. The Persian has returned to Mekran, bearing in a splendid palanquin a woman veiled and closely guarded, who is received into the harem of the khan after he had embraced her form in the sight of many servants. In this we read my own rejection, the failure of all our clever plotting. The harem, then, was not made beautiful for me, but for this strange woman whom the Persian brings to warm the cold heart of Ahmed Khan. Is she beautiful? Is she young and winning? Has she charms to delight the senses? Then why should she be chosen before me—the daughter you yourself have declared to be incomparable? Answer, you man of spies— spies so impotent that they cannot penetrate the secrets of the harem!"

"It is all a deep mystery, my Maie," sighed the vizier, solemnly stroking his beard. "But let us not be disheartened. There is room in the khan's harem for more than one woman."

"Unless Maie is first, there is no room for her in any man's harem," she retorted, proudly. "Have done, my father, with thoughts of Ahmed Khan. Our Kasam is assembling an army. Perhaps it is not too late to bargain with him for our support."

"Not long ago," said the vizier, slowly, "we rejected Kasam."

"The more reason that he will be eager to make a compact with us. We can open to him the gates of Mekran."

"A day or two ago," continued the vizier, "the Prince came out from his camp and met the American women who ride with Dirrag each morning. He conversed long and tenderly with the dark haired one. My spy saw all from a thicket on the hillside."

Maie's dainty face became grave and thoughtful.

"It is difficult to estimate the power of these American women," she said, after a pause. "Only yesterday I feared they might win the favor of Ahmed Khan; yet it seems I was wrong, for another has been received into his harem. Kasam's interest in them may be equally unimportant. He saw many such creatures in England, and cared nothing for them. Besides, he has a throne to win, and with it he may have—"

She stopped abruptly, and rising from her cushions approached a large mirror, where she examined her reflection with much care. Then she returned slowly to her divan.

"You are right, my father: no woman that I have ever beheld can compare with me in beauty of form or face—in grace or in womanly loveliness. The Americans could not amuse Kasam as I can. Let us think of them no longer, but send messages at once to the camp of the Prince. Without doubt he will accept our terms eagerly."

"I will do as you wish," returned the vizier, but with evident reluctance. "There is little doubt we can do better with Kasam than with the Khan, but by allying ourselves with the rebel we place our own necks in danger. I wish the Prince had a share of Ahmed's compelling will and cool judgment. When the armies meet Kasam may not win the battle."

"But the armies must not meet!" returned the girl. "With our aid Kasam can accomplish his ends by strategy. In battle the khan would crush him to the earth, but in cunning our Prince will prove the victor. Select your messenger with care—one whose death will not cause you to mourn, for we must trust no one with our secret. When he is ready to depart I will give him instructions."

"It shall be done," said the vizier.

"And now it grows late, and I will retire."

She made him a dutiful obeisance and left the room to go to her apartment.

An hour later, while the vizier slumbered, Maie stole away to the end of the garden and by the Gate of the Griffins came upon Allison, who clasped her fondly in his arms.

Next day David brought to the house of Colonel Moore the gossip of the city, telling of the return of Merad the Persian. The physician had been to Quettah for the most beautiful woman in the world, whom he had purchased for the price of ten thousand fillibees to grace the harem of the young khan.

The ladies received this wonderful tale with various comments. Aunt Lucy was very indignant that any female, however depraved, should be bought and sold like so many goods and chattels. Bessie wondered if the girl was really beautiful, and whether she was proud to have brought so large a sum of money. Janet said nothing, but listened with downcast eyes and flushed cheeks.

Somewhere or other Allison had also heard this gossip, and he took pains to quietly impress his sister with the fact that the incident fully proved them to have been mistaken in thinking they recognized the Persian on the day he had left Mekran.

"The doctor we knew in New York was an impertinent meddler," he said, when they could not be overheard; "but he wasn't the man to purchase women for the harem of a barbarian, you may be sure. We probably had our scare for nothing."

"Scare?" she exclaimed. "What do you mean, Allison? Why should you fear to meet—"

"Hush!" he interrupted, nervously glancing around. "They may hear you; and it isn't best, on your own account, to mention that name. I didn't mean that we need fear to meet him, but that he would be afraid to meet us. Is it not so?"

"You are talking riddles," she answered, coldly, and left the room to avoid discussing the matter further.

XV

SALAMAN

A solitary camel came into Mekran by the north gate, driven by a lean Baluch in a soiled yellow burnous and bearing upon its back a palanquin with curtains of faded silk. It ambled through the streets and knelt at the portals of the khan's palace, where the curtains were drawn and an aged priest cautiously descended.

Before the entrance was drawn up a company of warriors of the Tribe of Agot, who solemnly saluted the new arrival and pressed backward that he might pass within.

The priest paused to note their splendid dress and brightly polished weapons, eyeing them with the simplicity of a child viewing his first pageant. His countenance was strangely sweet and guileless, although not lacking in dignity, and his white garb was of spotless purity. But above his breast—the focus of every eye of the true believer—hung suspended a jewelled star that proclaimed him the Grand Mufti of the Sunnite faith. No wonder the awed warriors pressed backward before the great Salaman, who had come all the way from his retreat at Takkatu to visit their khan.

Passing through the courtyard and up the marble stairway the venerable priest stopped often to mark the luxurious furnishings of the palace. The building itself was scarcely equal to his own monastery, but the splendor of its fittings was in strong contrast with the simplicity to which he was accustomed. The slave Memendama preceded him, pausing at every turn to salam before his master's guest.

The ante-rooms were filled with sirdars and captains of the tribes, all resplendent in attire, as befitted the courtiers of a great khan. Within one alcove sat Agahr the Vizier, in deep converse with a group of greybeards who were evidently officers of rank. These also rose to bow before the priest, and Salaman stopped to read the vizier's countenance with curious intentness. When he had passed Agahr looked after him with a troubled face, and the others, exchanging significant glances, left him and walked away.

At last Memendama stopped beside a portiere which he drew aside to allow the priest to enter. It was the private apartment of the khan.

Salaman, stepping within the small room, gave a shrewd glance around and allowed the semblance of a smile to flit across his grave features. The place was well lighted with high windows, although the afternoon already waned, but the walls and floor were bare and the furniture almost severe in character. Beside a wooden bench knelt the Khan, his head resting upon his outstretched arms and his body without motion.

The priest's glance was almost tender as he softly crossed the chamber and seated himself within the embrasure of a window. The silence remained unbroken.

After a time the Khan moved and raised his head, fixing his eyes upon the white-robed priest. There was no start of surprise in his gaze. Very gently he arose, knelt again before Salaman and kissed with humility the hem of the priestly robe.

"You are here, my father," he said, "and I am grateful."

The priest laid his hand upon the bowed head.

"All is well, my son," he answered. "Allah and the Prophet have given you guidance, and your days are righteous." He paused a moment and then added: "We are pleased with Ahmed Khan."

Again there followed a period of prolonged silence.

Then the young man asked:

"You know of my troubles, father?"

"Yes, dear Hafiz. The American girl is here in Mekran."

"Is it not strange that she has come from across the world to the one place where I have found refuge?"

"The ways of Allah are good ways," responded the priest, "and He holds the strands of fate in relentless hands. Your life is just beginning, my Hafiz."

An eager look sprang to the young man's eyes. He searched the calm countenance of Salaman as if he feared it might belie the speaker's words.

"Do you bid me hope, my master?" he asked, in trembling tones.

A change came over the priest's face. His eyes seemed masked with a delicate film that gave them far-seeing power. The lines of the aged features grew tense and hard, as if deprived of all nervous volition. His head fell slowly forward until the white beard swept to his knees and lay upon them like a drift of snow.

Hafiz drew back, clasping his knees with his hands and looking up at the entranced mufti with expectant gaze.

"The deeds of men bear fruit," said the voice of the priest, sounding cold and unreal in the intense stillness, "and the sun of Allah's will ripens it all together and brings it from many parts to be heaped within one measure. The harvest is near, my son. Events will crowd one another like waves lapping the pool's edge, and from the midst of strife and bloodshed I see you rising calm and serene, with the mark of our gracious Prophet upon your brow. . . The Voice of Allah whispers in my ears. . . and all is well!"

Silence followed, and neither moved. A shadow crept over the windows, slowly dimming the light. An hour passed, and another. The room was dark now, and scarcely could the Khan discern the form of the priest seated before him. Blackness fell, and the stillness of death remained. From a neighboring minaret the hours chimed sweetly but all unheeded.

Then came a gleam of silver, striking aslant the priest's face and crossing the room like a solid bar, its end melting against the further wall. The bar grew and spread as the moon rose higher, and soon the entire room was flooded with a mellow light that rendered every object distinctly visible.

As if the radiance brought life in its dancing beams the aged mufti breathed again and moved slightly in his seat. Hafiz, alert to mark the change, softly arose and went to an alcove, returning with a tray upon which was arranged a simple repast. This he placed upon a tabaret beside Salaman and then brought a bowl of water and a towel, bathing the hands and face of his master with a touch as tender as that of a woman. The priest's expression was normal now, but very thoughtful. He ate sparingly of the food, and afterward the Khan also tasted the dish.

Then Hafiz, having carried away the tray, lighted a small lamp, green shaded, and both men approached the table and sat beside it.

"May I ask of Ahmed, my father?"

"He is now of the Imaum, well favored of the Prophet, his comrade, and happy in pursuit of a divine solution of the mysteries."

"Here his gentle soul would have been cankered with misery."

The priest nodded. Hafiz, after a hesitating look into the other's face continued:

"I have placed a woman in my harem, father."

A smile reassured him.

"All is known to me, my son," came the calm reply. "But I must speak with you concerning the Vision with which Allah has just favored me. Your vizier is not a true man, dear Hafiz."

"I have feared as much, my father, though striving to win him to me by many favors."

"He plots for your destruction, urged to treachery by a maiden very beautiful to mortal eyes, but equally repulsive to the all-wise Allah."

"It is his daughter," said the Khan, musingly.

"I have seen a man riding from Agahr the vizier to the camp of Kasam. Listen well, my son, for the Vision was given me that you might have knowledge."

In low tones Salaman now described the scenes he had witnessed in his trance, and the Khan attended gravely to each word of the recital, frowning at times, then smiling, and at the last giving a shudder of horror as the catastrophy was unfolded.

Afterward he sat long in deep thought, exclaiming at last, with a sigh of regret:

"These are evil days, my father!"

But the priest's face shone calm and bright.

"No man knows content," he answered, "who has never faced despair. The blessed Allah gives us night that we may welcome the dawn."

XVI

The Abduction

Janet and Bessie had continued their morning rides with Dirrag, notwithstanding the unpleasant meeting with Prince Kasam, which, although duly reported by the warrior to the Khan, had not been deemed of sufficient importance to interrupt their pleasure.

But since then Dirrag had led them through the valley to the south and east, where the country was more thickly settled, and avoided riding very far from the walls.

However, on the morning following the arrival of the Grand Mufti Salaman at Mekran, Bessie pleaded with Dirrag to again take them up the westward slope, that they might once more look upon the camp of the Prince. Dirrag hesitated at first, but finally consented and turned the horses' heads in that direction. The steeds of Mehmet, he reflected, were the fleetest in the khan's dominions, and his own trusted cimeter would be equal to any emergency. Moreover, when a woman pleaded Dirrag's heart was water, and Bessie was his favorite.

It was a beautiful morning, and the sun had just risen to cast a golden glow over the distant plain, where the white dots appeared to their eyes in increased numbers.

"Kasam's army is growing," said Bessie. "Surely there are many more tents than there were before."

"The air may be filled with vultures, yet they dare not attack a living lion," remarked Dirrag, quietly.

"But why shouldn't Kasam himself be the lion?" she retorted. "Is he so much inferior to the mysterious Ahmed Khan?"

"The future will decide that," said Dirrag. "Those who know my master have no fear of Kasam of Raab."

After remaining a short time to watch the picturesque scene spread out before them they turned their horses to descend the hill. All three were busy with their own reflections, and had nearly reached the foot of the incline, with the walls of Mekran less than two miles away, when three mounted men who had been concealed in a thicket dashed out and, without warning, fell savagely upon the band. Two with drawn swords engaged Dirrag in fierce combat, while the third, coming beside

Janet, dragged the girl from her horse, swept her across to his own saddle, and then galloped away with his victim clasped tight in his arms.

Bessie, reining in her horse, sat as if turned to stone, for she recognized in the abductor of Janet their old friend Prince Kasam.

With dull eyes and set face she followed the flight of his horse as he bounded up the hill with his burden, nor could the growls of Dirrag, who was engaged in beating down the swords of his assailants with mighty strokes, distract her from the more astounding sight.

Janet, unable to elude the fierce embrace of the man who held her, did not waste her strength in useless struggles. But after the first surprise of her capture had passed away she managed to find her voice, crying out:

"Release me, Prince Kasam!"

"Never!" he answered, exultantly. "You are mine, now—mine forever! And no earthly power shall ever tear you from my arms."

"Where are you taking me?"

"To my tent, beloved, there to become my bride. Don't you know that I love you—love you—love you!"

He repeated the words at each bound of his great black horse, pressing her yet closer to his breast, as if a madness possessed him.

"Never will I wed you!" gasped the frightened girl, trembling in spite of her effort at control. "You are a coward to seize me thus, and you are mad!"

"Yes, mad with love," he answered in a desperate voice. "I cannot live without you, my Janet. Willing or unwilling, it matters not. You shall be mine, and mine alone!"

She turned and whispered a word in his ear. He laughed.

"So much the better, dear one. We shall not have to wait for a ceremony. This is not England, nor America, but wild, free Baluchistan, and I am master of a host. You are mine—you are mine—you are mine!"

He did not see a great bay speeding across from a neighboring grove to intercept his path. He was kissing the girl's hair, her neck, her shoulders; hugging her fast in his wild embrace and blind to everything else.

The man upon the bay sat motionless, his huge, muscular frame bent slightly forward to favor the flight of his steed and his eyes fastened upon the Baluch prince and his fair burden.

The minutes were few before the noble bay of Mehmet pressed upon the flank of Kasam's gelding; the abductor felt a stinging blow upon the neck that lifted him full from his saddle and set him headlong upon the ground; but as he fell Janet was seized in an iron grasp and torn from his arms, being instantly transferred to a seat upon the other horse.

The bay never paused in its rapid flight, but swerved and circled until its head was turned toward Mekran.

Janet, bewildered and stunned by the excitement of her adventure, for a time lay inert within the strong arms of her rescuer. Then, slowly and shyly, she turned her face to his, and meeting the look in his grey eyes she smiled happily and nestled her head against the man's broad breast.

And it so happened that Ahmed Khan leaned over and kissed the white brow of the American girl just as his bay bore them past the spot where Dirrag stood with gory blade looking down upon the two motionless forms he had slain. Bessie had tumbled from her horse and lay in a heap upon the ground, sobbing as if her heart was broken.

The warrior smiled significantly as he looked after the flying form of his master. Then he turned and, not unkindly, shook the weeping girl's shoulder.

"Come," he said, "we will ride back alone to Mekran."

XVII

David Sells an Important Secret

David brought the note, which he had received from the hands of the khan's Arab slave, Memendama. It was in Janet's clear script and read as follows:

"Do not worry about me in anyway, for I am safe and happy. Of my own free will I have become an inmate of the harem of the Khan."

Aunt Lucy gave a shriek and fell over backward upon the floor, where her heels beat a tattoo against the rug. No one paid the slightest attention to her. The Colonel stared straight ahead with stony eyes and a look of horror upon his face. The doctor stalked restlessly up and down the room with his hands thrust deep in his pockets, whistling softly to himself. Allison, stolid and unimpressed, lighted his pipe and puffed away with supreme nonchalance. Bessie had not yet recovered from the adventure of the morning. She lay face downward upon a divan and wept miserably.

Under these adverse circumstances Aunt Lucy's fainting fit vanished. She sat up and glared wildly upon the perturbed group.

"This," she announced, "is the result of travelling in heathenish and godless countries. We are ruined!"

Her brother waved his hand impatiently, but no one answered in words.

"And to think how that demure minx Janet has deceived me all these days and made me believe she was respectable! Oh, it is terrible."

"Shut up!" said Allison, rudely.

"You're a beast, that's what *you* are!" retorted the old lady, white with fury, "and a fit brother for your designing sister. And to think that I've got myself mixed up with such a scandal. An American girl the inmate of a harem! What will be said when this news reaches New York? And Colonel Moore an officer of the great Metropolitan Construction Syndicate!"

"See here, Lucy," warned her brother, "you keep mum until you know what you're talking about. Janet is as good a girl as ever breathed."

"Only de best gets into de khan's harem," remarked David, consolingly.

Aunt Lucy turned upon him like a tigress.

"It's your doing, I'll be bound," she cried. "You're a traitor!"

David winced a little, and studied the pattern in the rug.

"Now," said the doctor, "it strikes me you're getting nearer to the truth, except that David is too much of a fool to be a scoundrel, and so may escape suspicion. But I'm inclined to think there has been treachery in some quarter, and that Janet has been forcibly seized by the Khan. I wish there was an American or English consul in this forsaken town."

"Her letter says she went willingly," snapped Aunt Lucy, and the Colonel groaned at the suggestion.

"It was probably written under threat of death or torture," replied the doctor, positively. "These Orientals are equal to any villainy. Knowing Janet as we do, and believing in her modesty and truth, it is absurd to interpret her letter in any other light. What do you think, Bessie?"

The girl shook her head, wiping the tears from her reddened eyelids.

"I don't know, papa. There's some dreadful mystery about it, I'm sure."

"The thing to do," said Aunt Lucy, "is to appeal to Prince Kasam. I never trusted that young man very much, but he's been decently brought up in a civilized country, which is more than you can say for that awful khan. In the circumstances the Prince ought to be willing to help us rescue Janet."

The Colonel stood up and brushed the gray locks from his forehead.

"I'll find a way to get to Kasam at once," he said, in a harsh and strained voice. "In which direction did you tell me, Bessie, his camp lies?"

She rose and walked steadily to the Colonel, putting her hands upon his shoulders and looking full into his eyes.

"I have not told you all the truth of what happened this morning," she began, bravely. "It was Kasam and his men who first attacked us, and Kasam who bore Janet away while the others tried to kill Dirrag. Afterward the Khan appeared and rode after them, rescuing Janet just as they reached the top of the hill. Kasam must have been killed or dreadfully hurt, for we did not see him again. The rest happened as I told you. Dirrag cut down the two men and saluted the Khan as he rode by with Janet in his arms. I must have fainted just then, for I knew nothing of this; but Dirrag afterward assisted me to get home, and when I wept at the capture of Janet he told me to dry my eyes, for she had smiled when the Khan kissed her."

"Impossible!" cried the Colonel.

"Dirrag is very honest," returned Bessie, hesitatingly, "and he thinks the Khan carried her to his harem that she might be safe from Kasam. I will not say she did not object; but, Colonel, there has been something strange about Janet for sometime—something I could not understand."

"I thought she was happier," said the Colonel, huskily; "that she was learning to forget."

"She has laughed in her sleep," continued Bessie; "she, who used to be so sad and melancholy. And only this morning she sang an old song as we galloped away from the town, and semed as light hearted as a child."

The Colonel buried his face in his hands, and a sob rose to this throat.

"Oh, my girl—my dear little girl!" he murmured; "what can I do to save you!"

"Cheer up, Dad," said Allison, brusquely. "There's no use taking it so hard. What does it matter whether Janet's in a harem or anywhere else, so long as she's happy and content? My opinion is we're wasting our pity on her. She isn't the sort to write a letter under compulsion, and you know it as well as I do."

"Really," the doctor remarked, "I can't understand the thing at all. If the girl had ever seen Ahmed Khan she might have fallen in love with him. It's common report that he's a fine looking fellow. But until today they were perfect strangers. H—m! Let me see. Wasn't there some old romance in Janet's life—some trouble or other?"

"Yes," said the Colonel. "But that is past and gone—years ago. Yet she brooded upon it, doctor, and it may have driven her mad."

"I've detected no signs of insanity in your daughter," returned the doctor, rather nettled at the suggestion. "But Allison is right; there's no use borrowing trouble over the matter until we know more. Perhaps we shall think of some way to communicate with her, or to force the Khan to give her up. We seem absurdly helpless in this tyrant-ridden town, although were we in any other country on earth we might easily assemble an army and rescue your daughter by force of arms, provided diplomacy failed. Kasam seems as impossible as the Khan, for Bessie's story leads me to suspect he's the greater scoundrel of the two."

David had appeared ill at ease during this conversation. Now he rose from his seat and after a half frightened glance around announced in a timid voice:

"I haf a secret!"

"Has it anything to do with Janet Moore?" asked Aunt Lucy, in her sharpest tone.

"It iss a fine secret," said David, fixing his little eyes upon the Colonel, "ant it is vort' a t'ousand fillibees."

The old lady gave a snort of contempt, but the Colonel seemed interested, and as he shrewdly examined the Jew's face he noted great beads of perspiration standing upon his shiny forehead—a warrant that David, at least, was very much in earnest in his proposition. It was not impossible David had a secret, and that he considered it a dangerous one to disclose.

"Will you swear that your secret is worth a thousand fillibees to me?" he asked.

"Sure, most Excellency—if your daughter she is vort' so much money," earnestly answered the Jew.

"She is worth more," declared the Colonel. "Tell me what you know, and you shall have the price you ask."

But David only stood still and trembled, answering not a word.

"Bessie," said the doctor, "take your Aunt Lucy into the next room, and keep out of earshot. We must have a business conference with David."

When the women had gone the Colonel walked over to a desk and took from a drawer a long envelope filled with English bank-notes, which he carefully counted. They amounted to six hundred pounds. To these he added a roll of gold and brought all the money to David, placing it upon the table beside him.

"There, David, are a thousand fillibees, in good English and American money. It is yours if you can tell me how to rescue my child from the palace of the khan."

David reached out his eager hands.

"Not yet," cautioned the Colonel, sternly. "You must first prove that your knowledge is of value to us."

The man drew back, discomfited.

"I vill nod risk mine head," he said, doggedly, "unless I haf de moneys. Id iss more to you dan id iss to me. Gif me de t'ousant fillibees or I nod speak von vort!"

The Colonel returned to the desk and brought forth a revolver.

"You will tell me all you know," he said, "or you will soon be a dead man, and then you won't care for the money. And if you do not tell me the truth, if your secret is not worth to me this sum of money which you have demanded, you shall never leave this room alive. On the other hand, if you have not deceived me the money shall be yours. Take time to think it over, David, and be sure I will keep my word."

David trembled anew, and cast a sly glance at the doctor, who looked as stern and determined as his terrible friend. Because of the excitement of the moment Allison had allowed his pipe to go out, and now sat regarding the Jew with a cruel smile upon his handsome features. Evidently these Americans were not to be trifled with. David looked longingly at the money, and gave a sigh. He was fairly trapped, and he knew it.

"Most Excellency," he said, mopping his brow with a dirty red cloth, "tonight de vest gate of Mekran vill be open't to Prince Kasam ant hiss army. De city vill be surprised."

"Who will open the gate?" asked the Colonel.

David hesitated.

"Tell me!"

"De vizier," whispered the Jew, with pallid lips.

"Well, and what then?"

"De Khan ant hiss people vill rush out of de palace to fight; but dey vill not be ready to fight, an' Kasam vill cut dem down."

"I see. And then?"

"Vhile de city iss in de uproar I leat you by a secret vay into de harem of de Khan. You vill take de girl ant carry her avay."

"Very good. Are you sure you know this secret way, David?"

"Sure, most Excellency. I pait a high price to find it oudt. A t'ousant fillibees! Id iss too liddle, altogedder."

The Colonel took a key from his pocket, unlocked the cabinet, and drew out David's leathern pouch. Into this he stuffed the money— notes and gold together—and then replaced the pouch in the cabinet, locking it securely.

"You will be a rich man, David, when we return from the palace," said he.

David clinched his hands and an angry look flashed in his beady eyes.

"Id iss nod right!" he protested. "You Americans do nod play de fair way, at all. You ged my secret ant you keep my moneys."

"Only until we have proven you," replied the Colonel. "If you are true, David, you will be rich. When are the gates to be opened?"

"Ad midnight."

"All the gates?"

"Only de vest gade. De vizier, he vill trust no von bud himselfs."

"Then how did you know of the plot?"

The Jew was silent.

"It will pay you to be honest, David."

"De vizier musdt sent a man to de prince," he said, reluctantly; "ant de man he owes me two golt fillibees. He tells me hiss message to de prince, ant I cancels de debt. *Sullah ben cairno!* id iss vell I did, for I safe mineself moneys. Ven de man comes back he hass a fit unt dies. De vizier he iss a cleffer excellency—bud nod so cleffer ass Davit." He stopped to chuckle softly and rub his hands together; but suddenly he paused and cast a gloomy look at the cabinet.

The Colonel tossed him the key.

"Now you will know the money is surely yours," he said. "Keep the key yourself, David, for you are going to stay here with us until after midnight. If you guide us safely to the harem you may go free. If we find you guilty of treachery I will put a bullet through your head. But in either event the key unlocks the cabinet and the money is now in your possession."

David nodded and secreted the key in his bosom.

"I am true man," he muttered. "Id iss impossible for me to deceive so great an excellency!"

"We three," said the doctor, "will accompany David to the harem."

Allison grew red and uncomfortable.

"One of us, sir, should remain here to guard the women. Let me stay. Surely my father and you will be able to look after David and bring Janet home in safety."

"That is not a bad idea," returned the doctor. "There will be wild times when Kasam's army enters the city. It will be well for you to be on hand to protect Bessie and my sister from possible intruders."

This being arranged to the young man's satisfaction the elder gentlemen left the room to make preparations for their adventure, leaving Allison to smoke his pipe and keep an eye upon the slippery David.

When they were alone the Jew approached his companion and whispered:

"Tonighdt you vill be in de garden mit de vizier's daughter."

Allison's face flushed with mingled fear and anger.

"What do you mean by that, you scoundrel?" he exclaimed.

"Davit knows!" chuckled the Jew, wagging his head. "Six time—sefen time—you meet mit Maie vhen no one knows bud Davit. Tonighdt you go again. She iss very lofely—very beaudiful! Ah, yes. Bud do nod fear. Davit vill say nodding—if he iss vell pait."

"Well paid? So you intend to rob me, also, do you?"

"I am true man, Excellency. Your fadder should know; de vizier should know; bud Davit vill forget efferyt'ing if he hass a hundert fillibees."

"A hundred fillibees! I haven't so much."

"Fifty, den. Fifty fillibees iss so small for so big a secret!"

"Very well; tomorrow you shall have them," said Allison.

"Bud, most Excellency, suppose I shouldt remember tonighdt, ant your fadder ant de vizier shouldt know vot Davit knows? I cannod forget de secret unless I haf de fifty golden fillibees. I vouldt try, Excellency; I vouldt try hard; bud I could nod—could nod forget."

Allison pulled at his pipe and thought it over, while the Jew stood cringing and smiling before him. Then he drew from his pocket all the gold and notes he could find and gave them into Davids hand.

"You're making money fast, you dirty pig of a Jew," he growled. "But watch out that you don't lose it just as quickly. I'll get even with you before I'm through."

But David had other secrets, the thoughts of which made him accept the young man's threat with a good grace. With evident delight he concealed the money in the bosom of his robe. It lay next to the hundred fillibees which Agahr the Vizier had given him that very morning. And the key to the cabinet was also in his possession.

David sighed from pure happiness, and sat down upon a chair to wait for the Colonel and the doctor.

"De easiest t'ing in de vorlt to sell," he murmured, contentedly, "iss secrets!"

XVIII

The Vizier Opens the Gate

When Agahr entered his daughter's apartment that night the girl sat propped with silken cushions while a female slave brushed and arranged the folds of her glossy hair and another woman sat at her feet to anoint them with pungent and sweet-smelling ointments. A shaded lamp of Egyptian design swung from the ceiling and cast a rosy hue over the group, and the air was redolent of the spicy perfumes of the East.

Agahr stood before his daughter for a time in silence, searching her fair and composed face with much earnestness. The soft, languorous eyes met his own frankly and lovingly, and she smiled until the dimples showed daintily in her pretty cheeks.

"You are welcome, oh my father," she tenderly exclaimed.

He seated himself in a chair and waved the women away.

"You are about to retire, my Maie?" he asked, when they were alone.

"I am preparing for the night, dear one, but I shall not retire as yet. How could I sleep with our fortunes swinging with the pendulum of fate? This night we win or lose all."

He did not reply, but sat moodily studying her expression, and she moved restlessly and turned her face slightly to the shade.

"Yet there is small risk of failure," she continued, after a pause. "The Khan, secure in the strength of his loyal tribes, has neglected to prepare for immediate battle, and Kasam's host, once inside the gate, will carry all before it."

"And then?" he asked, gravely.

"Then Kasam will keep his promise, and make me his queen. It is the price we demanded for giving him his throne. And, through me, my father, you shall hereafter rule Mekran."

The vizier sighed and stroked his beard.

"Are you willing to become Kasam's queen when you know he loves the American girl whom he attempted to carry away by force? Will you be able, without his love, to bend him to your will?"

Maie laughed softly, clasping her jewelled fingers behind the folds of her hair.

"Let him love the American girl!" she answered, a touch of scorn in her voice. "While he dallies in her presence I will direct the affairs of state. Listen, my father, I have never loved Kasam from the first. Nor could that cold-eyed Ahmed Khan have ever won my heart. Yet to favor my ambition I would have mated with either one. The fates now favor Kasam, and if I cannot rule him through love I will rule him through cunning. The foreign girl will not stand in my way. In the harem of a khan are subtle poisons and daggers with needle points, and no dull-witted Western maiden can ever hope to oppose your Maie's intrigues."

Agahr stared at her as if afraid. The perfect repose of her features as she hissed the fiendish words struck a chill to his very bones.

"You are false as Iblis itself, my Maie," he said. "How do I know you will sacrifice me, also, to your great ambition?"

"Have no fear, my father," she returned, her low laugh rippling through the perfumed atmosphere. "You live but to please your Maie; would she foolishly betray her most faithful servant? We are one in all things."

Again he sat silent, the frown growing upon his face. Perhaps he had begun to realize, for the first time in his life, that all this loveliness before him breathed passion and sensuality, but no warrant of a soul beneath its exquisite outlines. His child was beautiful, indeed; so beautiful that he had worshipped her as an angel of paradise, sent to comfort and console his old age. He had longed to see her acknowledged above all women of Baluchistan as the brightest star in the harem of the Khan himself—the greatest pride and glory a father and a true believer could conceive. He had plotted and planned to this end without regard or consideration for others: even with an humble subversion of self. But she had given him nothing in return. Her very love for him was more calculating than filial. And he knew her furtive mind so intimately that he might well doubt her truth.

"Since you were a child," he said, musingly, "I have made you my comrade; more, my confidant. You were not treated like other women of Islam, but given the full freedom of my household. I have loaded you with jewels, with fine cloths from the looms of Persia, of Turkey and of China; with precious perfumes and cosmetics from Arabia. Your slaves are the loveliest maidens of Circassia and Morocco, purchased with vast sums to minister to your lightest whims. Even the harem of the Khan cannot boast a greater luxury than that which surrounds you. Yet you have dared to deceive me."

The last words were spoken with impetuous force, as if evoked by a sudden thought. The lashes that veiled her eyes flickered slightly the accusation, but she made no other movement.

His voice grew stern.

"Tell me, why have you favored a dog of an infidel?"

"I, my father? I favor a dog of an infidel? Are you mad?"

"It has come to my ears," he said, stiffly. "The young American who came here with Kasam."

Maie stared at him as if amazed, as in truth she was. Then her head fell back and from her slender throat burst a peal of merriment that was well-nigh irresistible. She sprang up lightly, dropping her outer robe, and cast herself with abandon into the old man's arms, clinging to his neck and nestling within his lap while her laughter filled his ears like the sweet chime of silver bells.

"Oh, my foolish, ridiculous old father!" she cried, while kissing his forehead and smoothing his beard over her bosom, like a mantle. "Has the serpent of folly bitten you? What monster of Agoum put such dreadful thoughts of your little Maie into your suspicious head? An infidel! Has the Prophet forsaken me? Were I lacking in any modesty— which Allah forbid!—would a daughter of Raab choose an infidel?"

Agahr held her tight, and his heart softened.

"The tale was brought to me, and I could not but doubt," he said, doggedly. "But I am very glad to find you innocent, my precious one. Forget the words, Maie, for they were inspired by a lying tongue—one that I will tear out by the roots at tomorrow's sunrise!"

He arose from his seat, clasping her in his arms like a little child, and carried her to a divan, where he gently laid her down. Then he bent over and kissed both her cheeks.

"I must go now," said he. "Midnight approaches, and I must be at the gate to admit Kasam."

"You will disguise yourself?" she asked, holding one of his hands as she gazed up at him.

"I shall cover my head with a cloak. Beni-Bouraz is Captain of the Guard, and he must know it is the Vizier who commands him to open. Afterward it will not matter who recognizes me."

"Be careful," she cautioned. "We must guard against treachery. Are you sure no one knows our plot?"

"The messenger who returned from Kasam is dead. Yamou attended to him."

She nodded.

"Then go, my father; and may Allah guide your hand!"

Slowly he turned and without further word left the room. The passage was dark, and he stumbled along, feeling his way, until he came to the draperies that hid his own chamber. Having thrust these aside he entered to find the room well lighted but deserted by even his slaves.

Thoughtfully the old vizier sat at his table and pondered well the scene just enacted within his daughter's boudoir. While in her presence he had seemed convinced of her innocence; but now the old doubts assailed him anew.

Presently his brow cleared. He reached out his hand and touched a soft-toned gong, and immediately the tall, dark figure of a Moor entered and made obeisance.

"Yamou," said the vizier, "David the Jew was here this morning. He had a secret to sell. He swears that my daughter meets the young American infidel in my own garden, entering by the Gate of the Griffins."

The black stood as if made of stone, not a muscle of his face moving.

"Have you known of this, Yamou?"

"No, my master."

"It may not be true. David declared they will meet tonight—just before the midnight hour. You will take three of the most trusted slaves and at once hide yourselves in the shrubbery at the end of the garden. Remain there until daybreak, unless the infidel should indeed come."

"And if he comes?"

"Kill him, Yamou!" said the old man, with sudden passion. "And if Maie goes to meet him kill her also. I'll harbor no toy of an infidel dog in my household, even though it be my own daughter!"

Yamou bowed and touched the cimeter at his belt.

"You shall be obeyed, my master."

Agahr glanced at the brutal visage of the Moor and hesitated, repenting already his command. But Maie had protested her innocence in no uncertain words. He would believe her. Should she prove false, the fate that would overtake her would be her own fault, and not to be laid at his door. But there! she was innocent, without a doubt. Her ambitions were too great to permit her to descend to so unnatural and foolish an intrigue. It would do no harm to wash the blemish of David's lying tales from his daughter's fair name by hiding the slaves in the shrubbery. If proof were needed, there would be the proof.

"You may go, Yamou."

The slave salamed again, and noiselessly withdrew.

Left alone, Agahr drew a black cloak over his dress, arranging the folds to conceal his face and beard. Then he crept through an ante-room and along a short passage to a secret door that led into a small garden. Crossing this open space he unlocked a gate in the wall and so let himself into a lane that ran past the grounds of his mansion.

The streets seemed deserted and the night was very dark, for a storm was threatening. But Agahr knew every inch of his way and without hesitation threaded the narrow streets until he finally reached the west wall of the city.

Above the gate a dim light shone through the windows of the watch tower, and the vizier mounted the steep stone steps and pushed open the door.

Upon a bench sat two burly Baluchi, earnestly intent upon a game of dice. At the far end of the room, half hidden by the dim shadows, lay a dark group of slumbering guardsmen.

"Ah-yah!" called one of the dicers, as he noted the presence of a visitor; "what is wanted at this hour? None can pass the gate till daybreak." And he calmly continued to toss the cubes.

Agahr walked up to him and threw back the folds of his cloak.

"The vizier!" cried both men, in a breath, and rose to their feet, saluting.

"Yes. Open the gate for me, Beni-Bouraz. I am to meet a friend here tonight."

"But, master—"

"Silence! Do as I bid you, Captain. Open the gate."

The officer bowed low. Then he walked to the end of the room and kicked two of his men.

"Get up, you dogs. His Excellency the Vizier commands the gate to be opened."

They got upon their feet, growling at the summons, and shuffled over to the windlass. Beni-Bouraz released the bar, and the men began winding up the huge chain that raised the gate.

As he noted this, the vizier turned to descend.

"Come with me, Captain," he said to Beni; "it may be necessary to hold the gate open for a time. I will myself give you the command to close it."

The officer followed him down the stairs, and when they had disappeared from the room a big guardsman arose from the group of sleepers and, still muffled in his robe, followed after the captain. Also the others arose, seemingly alert, and by the light of the torch exchanged grins with the men at the windlass.

When Agahr paused before the heavily-barred gate it had already ascended toward the arch far enough to admit a horseman. Presently, with a final creak that sounded very audible in the stillness of the night, the windlass stopped and the gate remained poised in the archway.

Agahr bent forward, and heard the soft pattering of horses' feet. The sound was repeated to the right and left, echoing far out upon the plains as if an army was awakening to action. Then the patter broke into a gallop, and a single horseman rode through the gate, a drawn sword clutched in his hand.

"Light a torch!" said the voice of Kasam. "My men cannot see this accursed gateway."

Almost instantly a light flamed up behind them, and its red glow spread outside the gate and showed the plain fairly alive with a host of warriors.

"Advance!" shouted Kasam, and waved his sword around his head.

Then a strange denouement came. The immense gate, suddenly loosened from the tower, fell with a crash, crushing beneath its weight those of the front rank that already pressed forward to enter. A strong hand seized the prince and dragged him from his saddle, disarming him at the same instant.

And then a mighty shout burst from many throats, sounding from all the length of the great wall as well as from the horde that clamored helplessly without. Torches flashed, tom-toms were beat with lusty strokes and the alarm gong sent its warning tones reverberating throughout the city.

Agahr the Vizier was astounded. Even his sacred person had been seized and his limbs bound fast with strong cords. It had all happened so suddenly that the old man did not recover his wits until he heard the cries of Kasam's host as it retreated before the hail of missiles descending from the wall.

Then he turned to confront the stern features of Ahmed Khan, and dropped his eyes before the gaze he encountered.

Kasam, also securely bound, stood with a look of sullen rage upon his handsome face, but proudly erect as ever.

"I am betrayed!" he muttered.

"I, also, Prince, was nearly betrayed," replied the Khan, in a harsh voice. "The fortunes of war, in this benighted country, are often nursed by the hand of treachery. Fortunately for the safety of Mekran, I was warned in time."

Kasam turned angrily upon the vizier.

"I owe this to you, I suppose!" he said, bitterly.

"My bonds will prove my faith," returned Agahr, with dignity.

The Khan raised his hand, as if to command peace. The red light of the torch upon his face seemed to soften its sternness.

"That your disloyal plans have come to naught," he said, in more kindly tones, "is due alone to the will of Allah. Come, Captain Beni-Bouraz; you may follow me with your prisoners to the palace."

XIX

IN THE GARDEN OF AGAHR

When her father had left her alone Maie lay still, for a time, in deep thought.

"It must be," she reflected, "that our dear David, in spite of my bribes, has sold our secret to my father. For tonight, at least, I have lulled his suspicions. And he will soon be at the gate to admit Kasam; so I fear nothing. But the little David must not be able to annoy me again."

With this came a thought whereat she laughed. Rising from her couch the girl went to a tiny cabinet and cautiously unlocked it. She busied herself there for several minutes, at times laughing softly to herself, but with no trace of merriment in the notes. Finally she clapped her hands to summon a maid.

"Bring here one of the slaves," she commanded.

The girl withdrew, but presently returned alone.

"There are no slaves in the house, my mistress," she reported.

"Indeed! My father must have taken them with him," Maie replied. Then, after consideration, she added: "You will do as well, Halima; nay, perhaps better. Do you know David the Jew?"

"Yes, my mistress."

"Then get your cloak and seek David out, wherever he may be. And, when you have found him, give to him this casket, Halima, with the greetings of the daughter of the vizier; and tell him it is a token of my faith in him."

She brought from the cabinet a small box, exquisitely enamelled and inlaid with mother-of-pearl.

"Keep it safely concealed in your cloak, Halima. It does not lock, but opens by pressing this spring—so!" The lid flew back, disclosing a quantity of gold and gems and a silken purse; and after permitting the girl to glance within she closed the cover, snapping it into place. "Now that you have seen the contents, my child, you will not care to open it again. Keep it well fastened until it is in David's hands."

The girl promised to obey, and taking the box started at once to perform her mission. It seemed to her a queer hour—the dead of night—

L. FRANK BAUM

to carry a present to a Jew; but the whims of Maie were past accounting for, and the duty of a slave was to obey without question.

Left to herself, Maie glanced at the hour-glass and hastily caught up the mantle which she had discarded the better to display her charms to her father. She wound the robe carelessly about her shoulders, pressed a panel in the wall, and gained egress by a narrow stairway to the gardens.

"It is very dark," she murmured, feeling her way along a path; "but so much the better. My Allison will not need a light to know that it is I!"

Onward she crept, turning the angles of the hedges with unerring instinct, until she paused beneath a group of stately siszandras where the shadows were even deeper than elsewhere. But her eyes, growing accustomed to the darkness, soon made out the dim outlines of a stone bench, and she stooped and passed her hands along its length until she discovered that it was vacant.

"He is late," she whispered; "or perhaps I am a moment early. He will come soon."

Languidly she reclined upon the bench, her face turned toward the carved pillars that marked the Gate of the Griffins, standing but a few paces away like silhouettes against the murky sky.

After a few minutes' lapse a key clicked in a lock; a stealthy foot-fall reached her ears, and the next moment a man knelt beside her.

"Ah, sweet one!" he whispered, clasping his arms around her yielding form and covering her face with kisses; "again for a few moments I may enjoy paradise with you by my side! I have been very impatient, my Maie, for this hour."

"Yet you are late, Allison." She spoke his name tenderly, and her broken English rendered the sibilant very charming in his ears.

"I may be a trifle late, little one, for I met several groups of men stealthily creeping through the darkness. I cannot understand why every warrior in the town seems abroad at this hour of the night."

She sat up suddenly, clinging to him.

"Which way did they go?"

"To the westward, all of them," he replied.

Somehow the words sent a chill to her heart, for she remembered her father's mission to the west gate. Could their carefully guarded conspiracy have been betrayed? She listened eagerly, but all about them the town lay still as death. It was not yet midnight.

Her lover's caresses recalled her to the present. Allison had drawn her closer beside him on the bench, and throwing back her mantle was pressing her passionately to his heart. Unresistingly she nestled in his arms, the dainty oriental perfumes that radiated from her body filling his nostrils with their ravishing odors and the soft contact of her cheek against his thrilling him with a joy akin to madness.

Words were barren messengers of love now; only the throbbing of his heart and her gentle sighs betrayed to the caressing breeze the fact that the bench was occupied.

Suddenly she shuddered, clutching at his hand so fiercely that her nails were imbedded in his flesh. A low moan escaped her lips, and then her grasp relaxed and she fell back limp and inert.

Filled with a nameless horror, Allison looked up. The sky had lightened, somewhat, permitting him to discern before them the form of a huge black, who held within his hand a dripping sword. Even as Allison gazed the weapon leaped back and came straight for his heart in a quick thrust. He shrank from the point, springing sideways, but could not wholly escape. A biting pain pierced his side. But now he was upon his feet, one hand pressing the wound and the other holding his revolver.

A shot rang out, followed by a scream. The black swayed and fell, but others rushed with naked cimeters to take his place. Allison leaned against the bench and fired again—and again—and again, a fierce joy filling his breast at the outcries of his victims, even while the blood surged through his brain and he felt the numbness of death creeping over him.

The shots from the revolver were answered by loud cries from the other end of the garden—that nearest the house. Torches flashed, sending gleams of light dancing over the flowers and grasses toward the silent group beside the stone bench. Then came Dirrag, bounding over the sward with a band of chosen warriors in his wake.

At the ghastly tableau which the lights disclosed they paused, looking on one another with horror in their eyes. And now the deep tones of the gong from the west gate smote upon the air, rousing with its brazen warning all the sleeping city. The far-away outlines of the wall sprang into flame, while the hoarse cry of a multitude rolled grimly out upon the midnight zephyrs.

In the garden of Agahr a grizzled warrior bent over Allison's unconscious form.

"I think, my captain, the American still lives," he said.

For a moment Dirrag did not reply. He was gazing sadly upon the lovely face of Maie, whereon still lingered the traces of a happy smile. But the dark eyes, inscrutable as ever, were wide and staring, and the warrior leaned over and gently covered the dainty form with the folds of her mantle.

Then he stood up and coughed, for the night air had gotten into his throat.

"Come along, you dogs!" he growled. "Let us report to the Khan. The conspirator he sent us to arrest has escaped him."

"And the American?" asked a man.

"Oh, the American?" Dirrag hesitated, wondering how his master would desire him to act. "Well, bring the infidel dog along with you," he said.

XX

The Girl in the Harem

David was in high spirits. True, these absurd Americans had virtually made him a prisoner in their house until his services were required to lead them to the harem of the khan; but he had been clever enough to arrange all his plans beforehand. Now, as he sat in the dim room awaiting the hour of action, he felt he had good reason to congratulate himself. The service of the vizier had been especially remunerative, for in addition to his liberal pay as a spy he had that morning received from Maie a large sum to keep her secret, with a promise of more to follow, and then he had secured an equal sum from Agahr for betraying his daughter's secret. Was that not clever? Allison, also, who now sat opposite him silently smoking and at times stealthily glancing at his watch, had contributed much money for the preservation of a secret that was a secret no longer. There were three good strings to that bow, thought David, chuckling delightedly. And now the old underground passage into the khan's harem, which the Jew had discovered long ago and feared he would never have any use for, had paid him richer returns than all else. Mentally he figured up his various accumulations, both in money and jewels, and decided he was too rich to remain longer in Mekran. He would return very soon to Kelat, where there was more room for enterprise; or perhaps he would go on to Quettah, or even so far as—

"Come!" said the Colonel's voice, its stern tones interrupting David's meditations; "we are ready."

Allison gave a sigh of relief, looked at his watch for the twentieth time, and knocked the ashes out of his pipe. He might be a trifle late, but Maie would wait.

"We will leave you to look after the women," the Colonel said to his son. "Both the doctor and I are fully armed and will be equal to any occasion. But if David is right, and the night attack takes place on time, I anticipate no difficulty in getting Janet away from the harem."

"Good luck to you," said Allison, standing up to yawn and stretch his limbs.

"Have you a revolver?" asked the doctor, as his eyes wandered toward the rooms where his daughter and his sister slept.

"Always carry it," said Allison.

"Then be watchful until we return. No one knows what may happen."

"I'll watch out," said the young man, carelessly. And then, as David led the Colonel and the doctor to the street by one door, Allison slipped out at another and ran as speedily as possible in the direction of the vizier's gardens.

David was short and fat, but he proved an agile walker, and the darkness of the night was no hindrance to his way. He led his companions through many black alleys, turning first one way and then another, until he finally paused before a small stone house that stood vacant and delapidated. Drawing a key from his pocket he unlocked the door and drew the others into a damp and close-smelling room.

A moment later he struck a match and lighted a candle.

"Now ve can see vhere ve go," he said, complacently.

The Americans looked around them with some curiosity. Although doubtless of considerable age the house seemed never to have been finished inside, or even occupied as a place of abode. Bits of the building blocks were yet scattered over the earthen floor.

"Vonce, in de time of Keedar Khan," said David, "a young kaid built dis house ant made a tunnel unner de grount to de khan's harem, vhere hiss sveetheardt vas liffing. When she vas nod combing de vhiskers of de Khan she vas hugging de young kaid; ant vhen she vas nod hugging him she vas combing de Khan's vhiskers. Id vas very nice arrangements. Bud von night de Khan called on de female vhen he vas nod expected, ant he cut de young kaid ant de girl both into slices before he enquired how de feller got into de harem. Id vas all very careless of de Khan; but he had a bad temper. So de tunnel vas neffer used again until I find it oudt a couple year ago. I buy de place cheap because de mans vot owned it neffer looked to find a tunnel. Ant now id iss very handy for us, ant very cheap for a t'ousant fillibees. Come—I show you."

Chuckling softly, the Jew led the way through a narrow passage and down a few steps into a sort of underground cellar at the rear. Here, in one corner, a flagstone stood on edge, disclosing another flight of steps. Down these David proceeded without hesitation, the Americans following closely at his heels. Then came a damp, ill-smelling tunnel, so low that only David could traverse it without bending down. The candle lighted the way only a few steps in advance, and numerous rats scurried from their path as they slowly advanced.

It seemed like a never-ending journey; but, just as the Colonel was about to protest, the passage suddenly widened and grew higher, and the light of the candle fell upon a cedar panel let into the wall before them.

"Have you the key, David?" whispered the doctor.

"Id iss no key; id iss a spring," replied the Jew. "Vod time iss id now?"

The Colonel looked at his watch. It was nearly midnight.

"Shall we risk entering, doctor?" he asked; "or shall we wait for the alarm?"

"I doubt if we could hear an alarm where we are," was the answer. "Let us go in."

David's self-possession seemed suddenly to desert him.

"I iss no Moslem," said he, beginning to tremble; "but I respect de harem. Id iss to die if one iss caught. Davit vill stay here ant vait for you."

The doctor locked his fingers fast in the Jew's collar.

"You'll come with us," he declared. "Open the door, David!"

Perhaps David did not intend to obey so readily. He had scarcely touched his quivering forefinger to the dull metal of the spring when a sharp click was heard and the door moved and swung outward.

A gleam of light saluted them, half dazzling their eyes, and the group remained motionless, staring wonderingly at the scene the open panel disclosed. Perhaps the Colonel had expected to see in the khan's harem a mass of silken draperies, luxurious couches and priceless rugs, while scowling black eunuchs guarded with their naked swords a group of henna-dyed, be-painted and bespangled girls. Instead, he looked upon a scene that somehow reminded him of home. The furnishings were of an oriental character, it is true, but they were simple and in good taste, and an undefinable air of refinement pervaded the room.

Beside a table on which stood a bronze lamp sat a middle-aged lady with a beautiful face and sweet gray eyes. She was robed in a conventional European gown and seemed to be engaged, when so suddenly interrupted, in reading a well worn copy of the New York Herald. At her feet, upon a low stool, sat Janet, listlessly sewing upon some trifle that rested in her lap. On the other side of the table, his dark eyes fixed upon his work, sat the man we as yet know only as Merad, the Persian physician, busily engaged in writing.

At the abrupt opening of the panel, the existence of which was evidently unknown to them, the startled group turned wondering eyes upon the intruders, who seemed fully as astonished as themselves.

"God bless me!" cried the Colonel, partly recovering himself and stepping within the room. "Can it be you, Mrs. Osborne, in this impossible place?—And you, too, doctor!"

"Why, father! How did you ever get here?" exclaimed Janet, springing up to give him a warm embrace and a kiss.

And then the Colonel remembered, and a frown came over his face, succeeded by a puzzled expression.

"Isn't this the khan's harem?" he asked.

"I believe so," returned Janet, laughing. And then Mrs. Osborne, with old-fashioned courtesy, came forward and offered the Colonel her hand, smiling pleasantly into his staring eyes. The man, also, rose from his seat to shake hands with both the Colonel and the doctor, the latter gentleman seeming to be more amused than surprised at the encounter.

"You have taken us somewhat by surprise, but you are welcome," said Merad, in his deep, dignified tones, but speaking perfectly the English language. "I can appreciate your amazement at finding us in this place, for while we knew of your presence in Mekran, you were doubtless unaware that Mrs. Osborne and I are guests at the khan's palace."

"I—I can't understand it!" gasped the Colonel.

"Janet, my dear," said Mrs. Osborne, "will you try to find chairs for our friends?"

"Dear me!" exclaimed the doctor, looking around him rather nervously, "we came here to rescue Janet from the toils of an Eastern harem, and this is the most civilized looking place I've found in all Baluchistan. What does it all mean?"

"Permit me," said Janet, saucily, "to introduce you to the mysterious veiled lady who was reputed to be the most beautiful woman in the world," and she waved a hand toward Mrs. Osborne. "I will acknowledge that she is the most beautiful, but, daddy dear, I am myself the queen of the harem, and His Highness the Khan's favorite wife—being at present the only one!"

The Colonel's face expressed horror and grief.

"I—I don't understand," he muttered, vacantly.

"The explanation is very simple," replied Dr. Osborne. "My son Howard, who was at one time your private secretary, is at present Khan of Mekran."

A sudden stillness succeeded this announcement, and then a look of comprehension stole over the Colonel's face. He rose from his chair and drew himself up with cold dignity.

"Then, sir, I demand to know what my daughter is doing in the house of the scoundrel who swindled me seven years ago? As for her statement that she is his wife, that is, of course, a lie!"

The Persian confronted him with folded arms, looking down upon the Colonel from his superior height with the same intent and compelling force in the dark eyes that had awed the native assemblage at the death-bed of Burah Khan.

"Howard Osborne is not a scoundrel," he said.

"He is worse than that!" roared the choleric colonel, now beside himself with anger; "he is a thief, a forger and a coward. He signed my name for twenty thousand dollars, and ran away with the money. I have never seen his face from that day to this."

"It is true that my son left New York with this stigma attached to his name," said the other, calmly. "But he did it to save you, Piedmont Moore, from a still greater humiliation, although I vainly pleaded with him to consider his own family before yours."

"What do you mean?" demanded the Colonel, plainly staggered at this statement.

Merad, hesitating for the first time, glanced at his wife, who shook her head pleadingly for him to hold his peace. But Janet sprang forward and stood erect beside him.

"Tell him!" she cried, defiantly. "The infamous secret has been kept too long."

Then Merad spoke in a low, clear voice.

"Your own son was the forger," he said.

"It's a lie!" shouted the Colonel, shrinking back, nevertheless, from the Persian's calm gaze.

"It is true. The money saved Allison from shame and exposure; so Howard dared not force him to return it. But the bank, being the direct victim of the forgery, placed the matter in the hands of the detective police. The toils were closing slowly but surely around your son when Howard, seeing no other way to save you, and tenderly loving the sister of the real criminal, whose heart he feared would be broken at the disclosure of her brother's infamy, decided to save you all by acknowledging himself the forger. It was a rash idea, hastily conceived and executed in a panic of fear, for the detectives were close upon the trail. He left me a note, telling me the whole truth and begging me not to betray Allison, for he had fled the country and would never return. Well knowing that he did not realize the consequences of his generous act, his mother and I set out to follow him, and for seven long years we have striven in vain to regain our lost son. I will not bore you, Colonel Moore, with a recital of our anxieties and sufferings—borne on your account; but I think it ill becomes you to revile the name of Howard Osborne. Rather should you fall at his feet in gratitude for one of the most noble and unselfish acts any man has ever performed."

The impressive and convincing tones carried with them the warrant of truth. The Colonel fell back upon his chair, covering his face with his hands, and Janet knelt beside him, her arms around his neck and her cheek to his, striving silently to comfort him. And while they remained thus, with little David gaping in the frame of the panel and still holding the flickering candle above his head, the door of the apartment suddenly opened and Ahmed Khan strode in.

One look into the grave faces of the group before him warned the ruler of Mekran that a crisis had arisen. Janet arose and stole swiftly to his side, and he placed an arm around her with a reassuring smile. The Colonel looked up, and meeting the calm grey eyes of Howard Osborne he seemed shaken with a fury of doubt and rage.

"It is all false!" he cried, springing to his feet. "I am being tricked and deceived—even by my own daughter. This fellow is no Khan of Mekran, but a fugitive from American justice, masquerading as a native of Baluchistan. The forger of seven years ago is the impostor of today! Come to me, Janet. That man is not worthy to touch you."

"Worthy or unworthy," said the girl, clinging yet closer to the Khan, "my place is by his side. We were married seven years ago, before he left America. I am his wife, father!"

XXI

The Chamber of Death

The silence that followed Janet's declaration was broken by the tramp of feet along the connecting passage, followed by an abrupt knock upon the door.

The Persian opened it, glanced without, and then stood aside.

"Bring him in, Dirrag," he said.

Slowly the little band of warriors entered, bearing between them a limp form which they laid gently upon a couch.

The Colonel's face, as his staring eyes fell upon his son, was gray and haggard, but the old gentleman seemed to have exhausted his capacity for being surprised. Mrs. Osborne, with a shudder and a sympathetic moan, turned away weeping, but Janet crept close to the couch and gazed in mingled fright and horror upon her brother's motionless form.

"Is he dead?" asked the Colonel, hoarsely.

"Not yet," replied Dr. Warner, his hand on Allison's heart; "but he is dying."

"Where did you find him, Dirrag?" asked the Khan, in a quiet voice.

"In the vizier's garden, your Highness. He was attacked by Agahr's slaves, who likewise slew their master's own daughter, Maie."

The wounded man groaned, slightly moving his head.

"Stand back, all of you!" commanded the Colonel, with a sudden accession of his old brave spirit. And as they obeyed he himself approached the couch, a look of stern resolution upon his face. "Allison must speak, he must clear up this mystery before he dies."

The Persian motioned all the warriors save Dirrag to leave the room. Then he drew from his robe a small phial and forced its contents between Allison's set lips.

In a moment the young man groaned again, and then slowly opening his eyes, gazed vacantly upon the group around him.

"Allison," said his father—firmly, but in a tone less harsh than before—"here is Howard Osborne, whom I always have accused of forging, seven years ago, my check for twenty thousand dollars. He claims that he is innocent."

Allison moved restlessly, his eyes wandering from face to face as if in search of someone who was not present.

"I—I believe Howard is innocent," he answered, with much difficulty.

"Who was the culprit, then?"

The wounded man stared back into his eyes, but made no reply.

"They say you are dying, my son," continued the old man, gently, "and if you have done wrong—if you have ever deceived me—now is the time to confess all, and clear the name of an innocent man."

Allison made a motion with his hand, wearily.

"Where is Maie?" he asked, "and why do you keep the place so cursed dark?"

The doctor placed an arm under his head, raising it slightly.

"Tell me, Allison," pleaded the Colonel, "who forged that paper? Who was it, my son?"

"Why,—I did it, father.—It's all over, now—only twenty thousand—not worth—fussing about. Maie! Are you there, my Maie?"

With the words he made an effort to rise, and a crimson stream gushed from his mouth and nostrils. The doctor laid him back upon the cushions, while the Persian sought to stay the hemorrhage with his handkerchief. But Allison was spent. His limbs twitched nervously once or twice, and after that he lay still.

The harem of the Khan had become a chamber of death.

XXII

By the Hand of Allah

The events of this fateful night, numerous though they had been, were not yet ended.

Leaving the women to care for the dead man the Khan had withdrawn to his state apartment, taking with him the Persian, Dr. Warner and Colonel Moore, as well as David the Jew.

"It is best that all mysteries and misunderstandings be cleared up at once," said the young ruler, when his guests had been seated. "The hour is late, but I believe you will prefer not to rest until you have become acquainted with the facts that explain my presence here as the Khan of Mekran. But there are others in the palace who are entitled to hear the story, and with your permission I will ask them to join us."

The Colonel nodded consent. He was yet too dazed by the appalling tragedy of the hour to command more than a listless interest in these consequent proceedings. Dr. Warner was grave and thoughtful, but seemed to realize intuitively that fate had been kind to his old friend in removing Allison from his life. After the first shock of grief had passed the Colonel himself would acknowledge this. The boy had been a thorn in his side for many years.

"Dirrag," said the Khan, "tell Captain Beni-Bouraz to unbind his prisoners; and do you lead them here to me."

They sat in silence until the command was obeyed, and Kasam and the aged vizier entered the room.

The Prince carried himself rather better in misfortune than when free to direct his own actions. He appeared composed and dignified, accepting his fate with a stout heart and seemingly without desire to bemoan the triumph of his enemy. Agahr's face was sternly set. What his thoughts might be none could tell.

The Khan greeted his prisoners courteously, and waited until they had seated themselves before he began to speak.

"Gentlemen," said he, addressing the entire group, "events have occurred this night which render it necessary that you be made acquainted with some portions of my life history that you are now ignorant of. A few minutes ago Colonel Moore accused me of being an impostor, because seven years ago he knew me in America as Howard Osborne."

Kasam gave a start at these words.

"I have never believed you were a Baluch," he said, scornfully. "You were foisted upon us by that false mufti of Mehmet, Salaman, to further some interest of his own."

"It is true that I am not the son of Burah Khan," responded the other, in even tones. "My father is Dr. Merad Osborne, known to the people of Mekran as a Persian physician, and now here to verify my statement."

All eyes were turned upon the dark visage of the tall physician, seeking in vain a resemblance between the two men that would lend truth to the astonishing assertion.

Merad smiled.

"I will tell you my story," he said, "and then you will understand us better."

"I, for one, do not care to hear it," exclaimed Kasam, with scarcely suppressed eagerness. "If this man is no son of Burah Khan, he stands before us a fraudulent usurper, and the throne of Mekran belongs to me!"

"Not so," answered a clear voice, speaking in English, and the white-robed priest of Takkatu pressed through the group and stood before the Prince. "Ahmed Khan sits upon his throne by a better right than you can ever boast, Prince Kasam of Raab!"

Kasam was about to retort angrily, but he marked the jewelled star upon Salaman's breast and controlled himself to bow low before the emblem. England had not wholly driven out of the young Baluch's heart the faith of his fathers.

"Your words are strange, my father," he murmured, still somewhat rebelliously. "Is not this man acknowledged to be the son of Merad?"

"And who is Merad?" asked the priest, gravely.

"I do not know, my father."

"Tell him, Merad."

"I am the son of Keedar Khan," said the physician, proudly.

A cry of surprise burst from his hearers. Even the vizier, who knew no English, caught the name of Keedar Khan and looked upon the Persian with curious eyes.

"I believe," said Kasam, brokenly, "it will be best to hear your story."

The priest stepped back, giving place to the physician.

"Keedar Khan had two legitimate sons," began Merad, "of whom I was the younger by several years. My brother Burah was fierce and warlike, and realizing that I might at sometime stand in the way of his ambition and so meet destruction, I fled as a youth to Teheran, where I was educated as a physician by the aid of secret funds furnished by my father. When Keedar died and Burah ascended the throne I wandered through many lands until I finally came to America, where I met and loved Howard's mother, the daughter of a modest New York merchant named Osborne. In wedding her I took her name, my own being difficult for the English-speaking tongue to pronounce, and from that time I became known as Dr. Merad Osborne, a physician fairly skilled in the science of medicines.

"Our son grew to manhood and became the private secretary of Colonel Moore. In appearance he favored his mother, rather than me, having her eyes and hair as well as the sturdy physique of the Osbornes. Seven years ago, or a little more, the catastrophy that wrecked our happiness occurred. Howard disappeared, self-accused of forging his employer's name for a large amount. He left behind, for the eyes of his mother and me alone, a confession of his innocence, together with the startling information that he had secretly married Colonel Moore's daughter before the knowledge of Allison's crime was known to him. His youth and inexperience led him to believe that his sacrifice would shield his wife's brother and father from public exposure and disgrace, failing to take into consideration the wrong done to his girl-wife and to his own parents.

"I at once suspected that my boy had fled to the Orient, for he had always maintained an eager interest in my tales of Persia and Baluchistan, and knew I was a native of this country, although he was ignorant of the fact that he was the grandson of the great Keedar Khan. So his mother and I left New York, searching throughout the East in a vain endeavor to trace our lost son. At last we were reluctantly compelled to abandon the quest, and I settled in Kelat, where my fame as a Persian physician soon became a matter of note.

"It was in this capacity that I was sent for to minister to my dying brother, Burah Khan, who knew not that I was his brother. But I strove faithfully to carry out his will, and to preserve his life until the arrival of his heir. Then came from the monastery of Takkatu, where he had secluded himself, my own son, appointed by the Grand Mufti of the Sunnites to represent the successor of Burah Khan upon the throne of Mekran. To the great priest of our Faith," bowing low to Salaman, "no knowledge is barred, and from Howard's story of his father's life the Mufti knew the truth, and that he had a greater right, according to the laws of the tribes, to rule this country than the son of Burah Khan, who, also an inmate of the monastery, pleaded to be left to pursue his sacred studies at Takkatu.

"Of the strange coming of the Americans, through whom my son had been exiled from the land of his birth, I need not speak. The ways of Allah are indeed inscrutable, and Ahmed Khan has acted, during these past days of trial, by the advice of the great Salaman himself."

A silence followed this terse relation, which had sufficed to explain many things both to Kasam and to the Americans. David, also, shrinking back into his corner, listened eagerly, wondering if there was any part of the strange story that he could at some future time sell to his advantage.

"There is little that I can add," said the Khan, musingly, "to my good father's words. That he has always remained a faithful Moslem you can easily guess, and it was but natural I should embrace the creed of my forefathers. I found much comfort in the religious seclusion of the monastery, but it is nevertheless a great relief to me to be freed at last from the taint of guilt that has clung to my name. The only wrong I did in America was to secretly marry the girl I loved and then leave her to mourn a lover whom she might well consider faithless and unworthy. My only excuse is that I was young and impulsive, and my dear wife, who had never ceased to have faith in my honor, has generously forgiven me the fault."

As the Khan paused, Kasam the prince strode forward and held out his hand.

"Forgive me, my cousin," he said, bravely, "that I have been led to misjudge and oppose you. From this time forth Ahmed Khan shall boast no more faithful follower than Kasam of Raab."

Howard pressed the proffered hand gratefully. Then he walked over to the aged vizier, who had been a silent and puzzled witness of the scene, and touched him gently upon his shoulder.

"You are forgiven, and you are free, Agahr," he said in Baluch. "Go to your home, and may the Prophet shield your heart from the bitterness of the blow that there awaits you."

Agahr looked into his eyes.

"Is it Maie?" he whispered.

The Khan nodded.

"The hand of Allah," said he in kindly tones, "spares neither the high nor the lowly."

Agahr threw up his arms with a wild scream.

"The hand of Allah!" he cried; "no, no! not that! It was the hand of him that loved her best—the hand of her father!"

And muffling his head in his cloak he tottered slowly from the room.

XXIII

The Vengeance of Maie

To those who looked after Agahr with pitying eyes a slave entered, announcing a messenger for David the Jew.

The little man hurried away to the next chamber, where, dimly lighted by a swinging lantern, stood the form of a girl whose face was concealed to the eyes by the folds of a dark mantle. But the eyes were enough for David. He knew her at once.

"Halima!" he exclaimed. "Vy do you seek Davit?"

The girl drew a small box from her cloak.

"The gift of Maie," she said.

"Maie! Bud, dey tell me Maie iss dead."

"Of that I know nothing," answered the slave girl, all unmoved. "It is nevertheless her gift. I have been seeking you since before midnight, and but now discovered you were at the palace. Take the casket; and, mark me: here is the spring that opens it."

She drew the cloak around her again and with quiet, cat-like steps left the room.

David gazed after her with joy sparkling in his eyes.

"Id iss my luck!" he muttered, hugging the casket in an ecstasy of delight. "Id iss de luck of cleffer Davit! Efen de dead adds to my riches. Led me see—led me see if Maie iss generous."

With trembling fingers he touched the spring, and as the lid flew back he leaned over and feasted his eyes upon the gems and gold that sparkled so beautifully in the dim light.

Then the silken purse attracted his attention. He drew it out, loosened the string, and thrust in his thumb and finger.

Next moment an agonized yell rang through the palace. With a jerk that sent the gold and jewels flying in every direction the Jew withdrew his finger, glaring wildly at an object that curled about it and clung fast. Then he dashed the thing to the floor, set his heel upon it and screamed again and again in mad terror.

The cries aroused those in the next room; the draperies were torn aside and the Khan entered, followed by Merad, Kasam and the Americans.

David lay writhing upon the floor, and even as they gazed upon him his screams died away and his fat body rolled over with a last convulsive shudder.

"What has happened?" asked Kasam, bewildered—as, indeed, they all were.

The physician bent over and cautiously examined the crushed thing that had proved to be David's bane.

"It is a mountain scorpion," he said, "the most venomous creature in existence."

Maie's vengeance had survived her; but perhaps it mattered little to the dead girl that David's punishment had been swift and sure.

XXIV

The Spirit of Unrest

Two weeks had passed since the events just narrated, and peace seemed to have again settled over the isolated town of Mekran. Kasam remained at the palace, declaring himself a faithful adherent of Ahmed Khan, but although he had sent word to Zarig, the sirdar of Raab, who yet remained encamped with his warriors in the west valley, that peace was declared, the rebellious sirdar had refused to come into the city and make obeisance to Ahmed of Ugg.

All the Americans were now housed within the palace, and Aunt Lucy had come to revise and reconstruct her opinion of that whilom den of iniquity, the harem. But Allison's tragic death had sobered the good lady, as it had all of their little band, and checked for a time at least her garrulity and desire to criticise. There was no doubt of Aunt Lucy's democracy, yet it was amusing to note her pride in the fact that Janet was the wife of an Eastern potentate of the importance of Ahmed Khan. It would be a splendid tale to carry back to New York, and she had already decided to leave an envelope always carelessly lying upon her table addressed to "Her Imperial Majesty the Khanum of Mekran and Empress of Baluchistan." It would serve to amuse visitors while she arranged her hair at the mirror before coming down.

Kasam's wild passion for Janet had quickly evaporated with the news that she was wedded to Ahmed. The young prince was greatly subdued in spirit, and made no objections to Bessie's kindly efforts to console him. His position in the palace was necessarily an uncomfortable one, for he held no clearly defined rank in the household and there was no gift within the power of the Khan that it would be dignified in him to accept. Reared from childhood with the ambition of sometime becoming the ruler of Mekran by virtue of his royal blood, it was naturally difficult for Kasam to realize that this brilliant dream was past and he must be content to abandon it forever.

So he wandered restlessly in the gardens, with Bessie by his side, and accompanied the girl on long rides through the pleasant valleys, and might have been as happy as in the old days had he allowed himself to forget his disappointment.

Meantime Salaman, the Grand Mufti of the realm, remained the chosen companion of the Khan, who, notwithstanding the deference he paid to his illustrious father, leaned more upon the aged priest than any other of his friends. And thus it was that one bright morning they walked together upon a high roof of the palace, where none might interrupt their earnest communion.

"I have thought well upon your words, my son," said Salaman, "and examined critically your desires, striving honestly to quell my own inclination to oppose you. But I fear I cannot understand you wholly. What is there in this favored country—the land of your famous forefathers—that repels you, and inclines you to leave it?"

Ahmed paced up and down, thoughtfully weighing his words e'er he replied.

"It is, as you well say, my father, a land favored of Allah; yet the life here is the life of the lotus-eaters; or one of holy concentration; or even of idle dreams. Time has no wings in Baluchistan. We live, and lo, we die, while the sun shines fair as ever, the breezes rustle through the palms, the fountains still splash in their marble basins, and the endless chain of humanity creeps on from the cradle to the grave with uneventful languor. As it was a hundred years ago, so it is today; as it is now it will be found in future ages—merely Baluchistan, the home of a million contented souls, all faithful to Allah, all indifferent to earthly conditions outside their narrow limits."

"Truly, a paradise on earth!" said Salaman, nodding approval.

"In the West," said the Khan, a stronger note creeping into his voice, "a spirit of unrest is ever abroad. It impels men to do and to dare, feeding upon their brain and brawn rather than upbuilding them. They strive—strive ever, though erring or misdirected—putting their shoulders all together to the wheel of the juggernaut chariot of Progress and sweating mightily that something may be accomplished that was never known before. And in this they find content."

"Poor souls!" murmured the priest.

"Father, I am of these—my mother's people—rather than of those who rest satisfied with Allah's gifts. Here I may never be at peace. As Khan of Mekran I would overturn all existing conditions. I would plunge my people into reckless wars of conquest, build rails for iron chariots to speed upon—shrieking the cry of Progress throughout the land. Merchants from all nations would gather here to rouse the tribesmen to barter and sale, teaching them lies and deceptions now all unknown to their simple hearts. My father, I would be as dangerous to your people as a firebrand in a thatch. Let me go. Send me back to that country whence I came: the country that taught me unrest; the country where alone I shall find employment for an earnest heart and a strong right arm! Put Kasam in my place."

"It may be that you are right; that you know what is best for us all," replied the priest, sadly. "But you demand that I perform a difficult task. You are Khan of Mekran, acknowledged legally by the sirdars and—"

"Not by Burah Khan," interrupted the other, with a smile. "It was my faithful Dirrag who, dressed in the dead Burah's robes, enacted the Khan's part and acknowledged me before the sirdars."

Salaman gave a sigh of regret.

"True, dear Hafiz," he said, unconsciously adopting the old affectionate appellation. "But you are grandson of the great Keedar. You rule justly and by right of inheritance. And in the beginning you accepted the throne readily enough. What has caused your inclinations to so change?"

"I have found a wife," said the young man, proudly; "and she is an American. Without her I was content to merely exist. With her by my side I am roused to action. Hear me, father. Kasam will rule you better than ever I could do. His heart is here—where he was born. He will forget, as I never could do, the urgent prompting of that western civilization we have both known. Let Kasam be khan!"

Salaman came close to Ahmed, placed both hands upon his shoulders, and laid his aged head against the strong young breast.

"We have been friends, my Hafiz, and I have loved you. It grieves my very heart to let you go. But if I can compass the thing and bring the people to consent, it shall be according to your will. For life is brief, as you say, and Allah waits above for us both. And wherein would the charm of friendship lie if the selfishness of one should steal the other's heart's desire?"

For reply Ahmed gathered the speaker into his steadfast embrace; and so they stood silent and alone upon the housetop, with Allah's sun lovingly caressing the brown locks of the Khan and the silvery beard of the high priest.

XXV

Kasam Khan

I n the great throne room of the palace at Mekran were assembled all
the dignitaries of the nation—sirdars, captains, kaids; muftis and
mueddens from the mosques; civil officers and judges from the towns;
high and lowly officials of the royal household. Even the obstinate and
unbridled Zirag had yielded to Kasam's demand and, doubtless more
through curiosity than obedience, had left his camp to enter the city
and witness the day's event.

Of the nature or character of this event all were alike ignorant. They
merely knew they were commanded to assemble, and the authority of
the khan, backed by that of the Grand Mufti Salaman, ranking next to
him, was sufficient to bring them to a man at the appointed hour.

The press was truly great, even in this spacious hall of audience. Upon
a raised dais sat Ahmed Khan, arrayed in his most magnificent robe of
state. At one side, but upon a lower platform, sat Prince Kasam, and at
the Khan's right hand stood the Grand Mufti, wearing his decoration
of the jewelled star.

A silence bred of intense curiosity pervaded the assemblage. Even
Zarig, who, clad in his well-worn riding dress, had pressed close to
the platform, was awed by the dignity of the proceedings and glanced
nervously from Kasam to Ahmed and then upon the stately form of
the priest.

Presently the great Salaman stepped forward, offering a brief prayer
imploring the guidance of Moses, of Jesus, of Mahomet and of Allah
the All-Wise upon their deliberations. Then, drawing himself erect, he
addressed the people in these words:

"My friends and brothers, it is my duty to declare to you, as
representatives of all the people, that a great wrong has been done you.
It was not an intentional wrong, nor one which, having been discovered,
may not be fully redressed; nevertheless, you must hear the truth and
act upon it as you deem just and right."

He paused, and a thrill of excitement swept over the throng. In all
their history no such thing as this had been known before.

"The man who sits before you as Ahmed Khan," resumed the priest, in a cold voice, "came to you purporting to be the grandson of Keedar Khan and the son of Burah Khan, and thus entitled to rule over you. He is, indeed, the legitimate grandson of the great Keedar; but he is no son of Burah, being the offspring of Keedar's younger brother Merad, who fled to Persia an exile in his youth."

Notwithstanding the astonishing nature of this intelligence the assemblage maintained its silent, curious attitude. Many eyes were turned upon the calm and dignified countenance of Ahmed Khan, but no mark or token of unfriendliness was manifested in these glances.

The priest continued:

"Those among you who heard the dying Burah acknowledge this man to be his son, before all the sirdars, will marvel that my statement can be true. You must now know that at that time Burah had really been dead for two days, and that another falsely took his place. It was this lawless one who, masquerading as the khan, made the formal acknowledgment. For this reason Ahmed has never legally been your khan. He is not your khan now."

At last a murmur burst from the throng; but to the listening ears of the priest it seemed more a sound of amazement than of protest or indignation. Ahmed arose from the throne, drew off his splendid robe of office and laid it over the arm of the chair, disclosing to all eyes the simple inner garb of a tribesman of Ugg. With dignified mien he stepped from the dais to the lower platform and held up a hand to command silence. Instantly every voice was hushed as if by magic.

"Brothers," said he, "if I have wronged you I beg your forgiveness. Most willingly I now resign the throne to which I am not entitled, and ask you to choose for yourselves one more worthy than I to rule over you."

As he paused a cry arose that quickly swelled to a clamorous shout:

"Ahmed! Give us Ahmed for our Khan! None shall rule us but Ahmed, the grandson of Keedar Khan!"

Salaman turned pale at this unexpected denouement, which threatened to wreck all his plans. He strode forward and seized Ahmed's arm, dragging him into the background and then returning himself to confront the multitude.

Higher and higher the shouts arose, while the priest waved his hands to subdue the excitement that he might again be heard.

Zarig, scowling fiercely as the crowd pressed him against the edge of the platform, fingered his dagger as if longing to still this unwelcome homage to one of the hated tribe of Ugg; but so far as Salaman could determine there were few others who did not join the enthusiastic tribute to Ahmed.

But gradually the dignitaries tired of their unusual demonstration, and remembering their official characters subsided to their accustomed calm. The priest took advantage of the first moment that he could be plainly heard.

"Listen well, chieftains and friends!" he cried. "It is clear to me that your loyalty and admiration for Keedar's grandson have clouded your clearer judgment. Not that I denounce Ahmed as unworthy to rule, but that before your eyes sits one entitled above all others to occupy the throne of his forefathers—the descendant of seven generations of just and worthy rulers of this land. Brothers, I present to you one who is a native-born Baluch—the noblest of you all—Prince Kasam of Raab!"

Kasam, who until now had been ignorant of the purposes of Salaman, and was therefore as greatly astonished as any man present, obeyed the beckoning finger of the priest and arose to face his people with that air of proud dignity he knew so well how to assume.

Zarig shouted his name wildly: "Kasam! Kasam Khan!" and a few others, carried away by the priest's words, followed the sirdar's lead. But the shouts for Kasam were soon drowned by more lusty acclaims for Ahmed, and Salaman hesitated, at a loss how to act, while Kasam shrank back as if he keenly felt the humiliation of his rejection.

Driven to frenzy by the wild scene about him, Zarig sprang with one bound to the platform.

"No Ahmed Khan for me!" he shouted, and drawing a slender dagger from his belt he threw himself upon the American with the ferocity of a tiger.

But Kasam was even quicker. Before the multitude realized the tragic nature of the scene being enacted, the Prince had fallen upon his sirdar and plunged his knife twice into Zarig's breast. The man fell to the floor in a death agony, dragging Ahmed with him, while above them Kasam stood grasping the weapon that had so promptly saved the life of the man whom his people had preferred before him.

Then, indeed, a shout of admiration burst from the Baluchi, their impulsive natures quick to respond to the generosity of such an act. Ahmed, freeing himself from the dead sirdar, rose up and seizing the royal robe he had discarded flung its brilliant folds over Kasam's shoulders. Then he knelt before his preserver, and Salaman, prompt to take advantage of the diversion which was likely to turn the tide of popular enthusiasm his way, knelt also at Kasam's feet as if saluting him as kahn.

Zarig had accomplished by his mad act all that he had once longed for in life. The cries for Kasam grew stronger and more spontaneous, and Ahmed was able to quietly withdraw from the platform without his absence being observed.

Soon the people were as eager in shouting for Kasam as they had been for Ahmed, and Salaman lost no time in completing the ceremony that established the heir of seven generations of rulers firmly upon the throne.

Janet met her husband at the entrance to the harem, where he had hurried as soon as he could escape from the hall.

"Well, how did it end?" she asked. "They terrified me, at first, with their cries for Ahmed Khan."

"They terrified me, too, sweetheart," he answered lightly. "But my cousin Kasam is truly made of the right stuff, and turned the tide in the nick of time. Now then, join me—all together, dear one!—hurrah for Kasam Khan!"

And as their voices died away an answering shout, grave and stern, came like an echo from the great audience chamber:

"Kasam Khan!"

Her Serene Highness the Khanum

Never had a better equipped caravan left the gates of Mekran to cross the Gedrusian Desert in the direction of Kelat and civilization. The palanquins of the dromedaries were so comfortable that Aunt Lucy declared she felt as if on shipboard. The horses were the finest the famous monastery of Mehmet had ever bred; the pack animals bore tents and material for the nightly camp that would have been worthy the great Alexander himself, and everything that might contribute to the comfort and even luxury of the travellers had been provided with a liberal hand. Here were the twenty Afghans, too, glad of the chance to return to their own country again; but of the former party some were missing and some had been added.

Dirrag was the guide, this time, and the faithful fellow lost no opportunity to implore Howard Osborne to take him along to America. "Your Highness will need a bodyguard," he argued, "so why not take me, whom you may trust?"

"We don't use body guards in America, Dirrag," was the laughing answer.

"But we have such things as true friends—when we can get them," said Janet, brightly; "so I shall insist upon having my old warrior by my side, wherever we may go."

"That settles it, Dirrag," announced the doctor; "you're half an American already. Heigh-ho! I wish I could go with you. But Bessie says I must return to her just as soon as I've bought the new furnishings for the palace and seen Lucy well on her way home. You may expect me to end my days in this jumping-off place, my dear Colonel."

"It's really a very fine country," declared Aunt Lucy, with an air of proud proprietorship; "and it's only natural, Luther, you should wish to live with Her Serene Highness the Khanum of Mekran and Empress of Baluchistan, who is your only daughter and my niece."

"Fiddlesticks!" said the doctor, laughing. "I really believe the only reason Lucy is anxious to get back to New York," he remarked to Dr. and Mrs. Osborne in a loud aside, "is to air her relationship with the Khanum. Oh, by the way, Colonel," turning to his old friend, "how about that railroad?"

"Bother the railroad!" growled the Colonel. "I'd forgotten all about it."

A Note About the Author

L. Frank Baum (1856–1919) was an American author of children's literature and pioneer of fantasy fiction. He demonstrated an active imagination and a skill for writing from a young age, and was encouraged by his father who bought him the printing press with which he began to publish several journals. Although he had a lifelong passion for theater, Baum found success with his novel *The Wonderful Wizard of Oz* (1900), a self-described "modernized fairy tale" that led to thirteen sequels, inspired several stage and radio adaptations, and eventually, in 1939, was immortalized in the classic film starring Judy Garland.

A Note from the Publisher

Spanning many genres, from non-fiction essays to literature classics to children's books and lyric poetry, Mint Edition books showcase the master works of our time in a modern new package. The text is freshly typeset, is clean and easy to read, and features a new note about the author in each volume. Many books also include exclusive new introductory material. Every book boasts a striking new cover, which makes it as appropriate for collecting as it is for gift giving. Mint Edition books are only printed when a reader orders them, so natural resources are not wasted. We're proud that our books are never manufactured in excess and exist only in the exact quantity they need to be read and enjoyed.

bookfinity™

Discover more of your favorite classics with Bookfinity™.

- Track your reading with custom book lists.
- Get great book recommendations for your personalized Reader Type.
- Add reviews for your favorite books.
- AND MUCH MORE!

Visit **bookfinity.com** and take the fun Reader Type quiz to get started.

Enjoy our classic and modern companion pairings!

Printed in the USA
CPSIA information can be obtained
at www.ICGtesting.com
JSHW082348140824
68134JS00020B/1956

9 781513 211794